WHISPERS OF FATE

HILIARY AMANDA

To the love of my life,
Your steadfast belief in me, along with your endless support and encouragement, has ignited my passion and inspires every word I write.
To my kids,
You inspire me to weave tales of adventure and courage and remind me daily of the beauty in life's adventures.
To my family and friends,
Your support keeps the shadows at bay, fueling my creativity.
And to all my supporters,
Thank you for joining me on this journey—your encouragement makes every twist and turn worth it.

WHISPERS OF FATE

The past is a fog on our minds. The future? A complete dream. We can neither guess the future, neither change the past. - Shams Tabrizi

But what if we could?

PREFACE

"Thank you for joining us, Mr. and Mrs. Lang. Your presence here today is greatly appreciated as we discuss your son Blake's recent behavior. We've noticed some concerning things and want to address them with you in hopes of finding a solution together to get him back on track."

His mother's face immediately shows offense at the mention of her son's behavior. The teacher pulls a piece of paper from her folder and slides it across the table towards the parents. "Take this drawing, for example. This is not what we expect from a well-adjusted ten-year-old in art class."

His father scoffs, and his mother leans closer to examine the drawing. "Perhaps what you're seeing isn't what he was actually drawing. Art is open to interpretation," she says defensively.

"Respectfully, ma'am, I believe we are all seeing the same thing here. And let's be honest, it's not normal. And that was just one incident among many. Last month in science class, Mr. Mini had prepared the students for a frog dissection. However, Blake snuck in before class and dissected several frogs on his own, playing with their insides like it was nothing out of the ordinary. It was quite disturbing. And yesterday during lunch, when the kids were eating pasta, he made a comment about how it resembled brains. When a girl at his table scolded him for being gross, he responded that he wished he could see inside her face."

Blake's parents sit in shock, their minds reeling with uncertainty. They are unsure how to process what they've just heard, let alone address it with their son. As they contemplate their next steps, Blake walks over to the table with a piece of paper in hand.

"Mom, look at what I just drew!" he exclaims with a huge smile. "Do you like it?"

She looks down at the paper and gasps in horror at what she sees.

I

CHAPTER ONE

Blake emerges from the depths of his parent's basement with a heavy sigh, ready to face another day at work. His thin frame belies his excellent health, a genetic rarity in his family. Both of his parents suffer from various ailments - his mother with crippling arthritis and a pacemaker, and his father with high blood pressure, high cholesterol, and diabetes. However, Blake's struggles are of a different kind, stemming from his introverted nature and low self-worth. Blake looks in the mirror, practicing the smile he'll use today before heading downstairs.

"Alright, Mom, Dad. I'm off to work."

"Did you pack last night's lasagna for your lunch?" His mom questions with concern as she turns the corner from the kitchen toward him as he walks toward the door.

"Yes, Mom."

The frail woman hobbles slowly, her arthritis causing her more pain than usual this morning. The lines on her face reflect her discomfort. She embraces him before he heads out for his daily bike ride to work.

"Mom, can you please make sure Dad takes his meds? You know how forgetful he's been lately. I don't want a repeat of the other day."

"Don't worry, I'll remind him; you shouldn't be worrying about us; focus on getting to work safely. Drivers are reckless and don't pay any attention to bikers."

Blake nods his head in agreement and closes the door behind him. As he descends the porch steps, he grabs his trusty black trail bike and sets off for his twenty-minute journey to work. The crisp morning air fills his lungs as he pedals away, leaving behind the familiar comforts of home for the challenges that await him at work.

On warm weather days, he prefers to bike to work. The ride calms his anxiety and helps him get in the right headspace for the day.

Blake once again finds himself daydreaming of a better life as he pulls into the parking lot of his office building. A life where he is better looking has more friends and is happier in general. "Some day," he sighs, putting the lock on his bike and shifting his bag. "It's going to be a good day, it's going to be a good day," he repeats under his breath as he enters the building.

The office is always bustling with activity. It's a smaller marketing company with less than 50 employees. All of which are friends and enjoy spending time together inside and outside work. Well, everyone except Blake. His awkwardness and introverted behavior never allow him to mesh with his co-workers. They all think he's weird.

Today is no exception. As Blake settles into his desk, he can hear the faint whispers and see the subtle glances his colleagues cast his way. He often finds himself thinking dark and sinister thoughts about his comrades, especially when they are blatantly making fun of him. No one knows this side of him except his parents, and they don't even know the full extent of it. He keeps it to himself because he knows society frowns upon getting pleasure from other people's pain or misfortune.

Ignoring the uncomfortable atmosphere around him, Blake focuses on his computer screen and dives into his tasks. He knows he's good at what he does—creating compelling ad campaigns and engaging social media content—even if his personal social skills leave much to be desired.

As the work day comes to an end, Blake finds himself engrossed in his work, the familiar routine of researching, brainstorming, and designing, helping to drown out his awkwardness in the office. He glances at the clock and realizes it's almost time for the weekly team meeting. Gathering his notes and taking a deep breath, he makes his way to the conference room, where everyone is already seated, chatting and laughing amongst themselves. He finds an empty seat near the back, quietly sits down, and tries to blend into the background.

The meeting begins with the team leader reviewing recent projects and upcoming deadlines. As discussions flow back and forth, Blake feels a knot forming in his stomach, knowing he will have to present his work soon. When his turn comes, he stands up nervously, hands slightly trembling as he plugs in his laptop to display his latest ad campaign. The room falls silent as his creation fills the screen, showcasing vibrant imagery and catchy slogans. Blake starts to explain his concept, but the bored looks and snide snickers cause him to stumble over his words, only creating more stuttering and embarrassment for Blake. After he finishes his presentation, the room is completely silent. Blake looks around the room at the blank faces. Axel lifts his arms in the air and lets out an exaggerated yawn. The room erupts into laughter, and Blake drops his head in embarrassment. He scoops up his laptop and makes his way back to his seat.

As Blake sits back down, the humiliation grows deep in the pit of his stomach. Their laughter echoing in his ears, each chuckle and snicker a dagger to his already fragile self-esteem. His hands tremble as he packs up his belongings, trying to ignore the pitying glances from his colleagues. The team meeting continues, but Blake is no longer mentally in the room. His mind is consumed with self-doubt and anguish, the familiar darkness creeping in at the edges of his consciousness.

He shakes his head in an attempt to ward off the thoughts that are forming, the edges of his mouth turning slightly upward as he silently entertains them. He desperately fights the urge to smile or laugh full-on while glancing over at Axel, who is still mocking him as Blake sits down.

"If only," he thinks to himself as a flash image of Axel in an ominous predicament pops into his mind.

Blake's heart races at the sudden and unsettling thought that crosses his mind. He tries to push it away, to dismiss it as a fleeting fantasy born out of humiliation. But the image lingers, growing more vivid and enticing with each passing moment. He can almost taste the satisfaction it promises, the sweet release of power over those who had belittled him for so long. As the meeting drones on, Blake finds himself consumed by a newfound sense of purpose, a dark and twisted desire to make his tormentors pay.

"Excellent work, Blake," Mr. Hayes compliments while patting Blake on the back as he passes by, making his way to the front of the room, snapping Blake out of his evil and intrusive thoughts. Mr. Hayes is the company's VP. He has known for a long time that Blake does not get along well with the rest of the staff. There is a wedge there that he's unsure how to patch. However, he likes Blake. He's a hard worker, and his work is always top-notch. He knows Blake has potential with the company, but only if he gets out of his own way.

Mr. Hayes clears his throat, capturing the room's attention. "I have an announcement to make," he begins, looking around at his team. As you all know, our company is on the brink of a major expansion, and with that comes new opportunities for growth and development." The room buzzes with excitement and anticipation as Mr. Hayes paces back and forth at the front of the conference room.

Blake's heart races with a mix of hope and anxiety. Could this be the chance he's been waiting for to prove himself? His mind races with possibilities as he dares to imagine a future where he is no longer the office outcast and where his colleagues recognize and respect his talents.

"As part of our expansion plans, I have decided to create a new position within the company," Mr. Hayes continues, pausing for dramatic effect. "This role will involve leading a special project crucial to our success in the coming months." He locks eyes with Blake, who sits up a little straighter in his seat, his heart pounding in his chest. Could this be the opportunity he's been yearning for, a chance to finally break free from the shadows of his self-doubt and insecurity?

"I believe this project requires someone with creativity, dedication, and a fresh perspective," Mr. Hayes says. "With that said, the board and I have discussed this position and promotion and have narrowed it down to two potential candidates: Blake and Matt. Blake's heart leaps with a mix of excitement and nervousness at the mention of his name. The room falls silent, all attention turning to him and Matt, who sits across the table with a smug expression. Blake can sense everyone's gaze on him, waiting for his reaction.

Mr. Hayes looks between Blake and Matt before finally speaking. "I have observed both of you closely over the past few months, and I believe either of you can take on this new role." He pauses, letting the tension in the room build. "However, there can only be one person to lead this project. We will give you two weeks to assemble a mock campaign and present it in front of the board, our CEO, and a representative from their company."

"This promotion is mine," Matt chides, bumping shoulders with Axel and sneering toward Blake.

Blake's stomach churns at Matt's smug demeanor, his confidence faltering in the face of such blatant hostility. He takes a deep breath, steeling himself against the wave of doubt threatening to consume him. This is his chance to prove himself, to show everyone - including himself - that he is capable of greatness.

All focus is on Mr. Hayes when he clears his throat, drawing the attention of the room back to him. He has a massive grin and is tapping his fingers together in excitement.

"Don't think that was the only exciting news I had to share today. I'm not leaving the rest of you out," he announces, his voice filled with enthusiasm. The employees lean in eagerly.

"Now, as sort of both a team-building exercise and reward vacation, I am taking everyone on a weekend getaway to the Blackfoot Wilderness Campground."

Instant dread wells up into the pit of Blake's stomach. The thought of being in the woods, camping for a weekend with his coworkers, almost sends him into an anxiety attack.

The room explodes with chatter and excitement at Mr. Hayes's announcement of the weekend getaway. Colleagues start discussing plans, sharing camping tips, and expressing their enthusiasm for the upcoming trip. Blake's dread only deepens as he imagines the awkward social interactions and potential for further humiliation in such a setting.

Blake slowly raises his hand from the back and clears his throat. The whole room turns to look at him. Blake rarely asks questions, and truthfully, most of the time, they forget he's even in the room. Mr. Hayes nods his head in the direction of Blake.

"I'm sorry to interrupt Mr. Hayes, but is this retreat mandatory?" Blake asks, obvious concern crossing his face.

While the VP recognizes Blake's question is more of a request not to attend, he really does want to help him fit it more.

"Yes, I want everyone to come on this trip. We will have an entire day of team-building exercises and adventures, and then we will have fun the rest of the time!"

Blake lets out an audible sigh, and several co-workers roll their eyes in his direction.

Blake's heart sinks at the thought of spending an entire weekend in the wilderness with a group of people who don't even like him. They will be fine, but he'll be the one who's uncomfortable the whole time. The idea of team-building exercises and forced socialization makes his skin crawl. His anxiety levels spike, and panic starts to set in.

With dread in his chest, Blake plasters a fake smile on his face and forces out a response, "I understand, Mr. Hayes. I'll be there." The words taste bitter on his tongue. He takes several deep breaths in an attempt to calm his racing heart.

Blake's heart sinks at Mr. Hayes's response, his anxiety reaching new heights at the thought of being forced into a situation that fills him with dread. He nods in acknowledgment, trying to mask his unease behind a forced smile. "And he's in the race to land that job? He's weird as fuck. No way is he getting it over Matt." Someone starts laughing. Dread washes over Blake like a dark cloud. The thought of spending an entire weekend at the Blackfoot Wilderness Campground with his coworkers is suffocating. His mind races with anxiety-inducing scenarios of being stuck in the middle of nowhere, forced to participate in activities that only serve to highlight his social awkwardness.

As the meeting ends, Blake gathers his things and makes a beeline for the exit, desperate to escape the stifling atmosphere of the conference room. He can sense his colleagues' scrutinizing stares following him; their whispers and hushed tones only amplify his discomfort.

Walking out into the cool hallway air, Blake takes a moment to catch his breath and collect his thoughts. But amidst the turmoil of his overthinking, a spark of determination ignites within him. He refuses to let fear dictate his actions any longer. This is his chance to prove himself, not just to his colleagues but to himself as well.

He hears the animated chatter going on all around him as everyone else makes their way to their offices.

Blake feels like an outsider, disconnected from their camaraderie. He longs to be included and be part of the team, but his fear is like an invisible barrier.

"It's gotta be time to get outta here," Blake mumbles, looking down at his watch. It reads four forty-eight. "Close enough." He stops by his desk to gather his things and heads toward the door.

As he exits the office and onto the bustling city streets, Blake can't shake the unease that gnaws at him. Unlocking his bike, he hops on and begins the ride back home. Usually, the trek home calms his mind and eases his stress. However, today, it's doing nothing to tame his thoughts. By the time he gets home, he wants nothing more than to go to bed.

As he opens the front door, his senses are greeted by the

delicious smells of his mother's cooking wafting from the kitchen throughout the house.

Blake drops his bag by the door and makes his way to the kitchen, where his mother stands over the stove, a look of concentration on her face as she stirs a pot of simmering sauce. The familiar sight brings Blake a sense of comfort, grounding him in the midst of his swirling thoughts.

"Hey there, honey. How was work today?" His mother greets him with a warm smile, her soft loose skin crinkling into deep wrinkles. Blake can tell she is trying to hide her obvious physical pain, though. She always does that; he can always tell.

Blake hesitates for a moment before replying, unsure how to describe his tumultuous day. He hates to worry her, so he puts on the same brave face he has every other evening. "Oh, mom, you know. Just another day at the office. How was your day? Dad doing okay? You look like you're hurting. Can I help you finish dinner?"

His mother listens attentively, her gentle presence a soothing balm to his frayed nerves. When he finishes speaking, she touches his shoulder and offers a reassuring smile.

"I'll be fine. Don't worry. Your father and I had a very relaxing day. Dinner will be ready in just a few minutes. Why don't you go wash up."

Blake nods gratefully, the tension in his shoulders easing slightly at his mother's comforting words. He gives her a quick hug before heading downstairs to wash up.

Standing in front of the bathroom mirror, Blake meets his own gaze, searching for some semblance of confidence within himself. He takes a deep breath, trying to steady his racing heart and quiet the doubts that threaten to overwhelm him.

After freshening up, Blake joins his parents at the dinner table, where the savory aroma of his mother's cooking fills the air. They eat in comfortable silence, the clinking of utensils and occasional murmurs creating a soothing backdrop to their meal.

"Do you want to play penny poker with Dad and me tonight?" his mom asks with a smile as she picks up Blake's plate from the table and stacks it on top of hers.

"I want payback for you taking all my change last week," his dad laughs.

"I'm actually exhausted tonight. I think I'm just going to go lay down."

"Oh no! Are you coming down with something?" His mother checks his forehead for a fever, concern crossing her face. He shrugs her off, slightly annoyed.

"I'm fine; I'm just tired. I'm not a baby."

The older woman takes a step back in surprise and nods her head. "Sure, honey, of course." She turns her back to him and walks toward the kitchen with the dirty dishes. A pang of guilt hits Blake in the heart.

"Mom, I...."

"No, it's fine. You go rest."

Blake watches her for a minute as she fiddles with something on the stove. Then, he turns his gaze to his father, who glares at him across the table.

"Dad, I didn't mean it the way it came out."

"All that woman does is take care of you. The least you can do is give her the respect she deserves."

"I know, I..."

"Don't, just go," his dad says quickly, his voice laced with disappointment.

A massive wave of guilt settles in his chest as Blake retreats to his room, his father's words echoing in his mind. He knows he should have reacted differently and shown more appreciation for all that his mother does for him. As he lies on his bed, staring at the ceiling, a mix of emotions swirls within him—

guilt, frustration, and a deep sense of unease about the upcoming weekend trip.

Despite being utterly exhausted, sleep eludes him as he repeatedly replays the events of the day in his mind. The thought of the camping trip looms over him like a dark cloud, casting a shadow of anxiety that refuses to dissipate. Not to mention how much he really wants to beat Matt out for the new position. He has worked so long and hard for this company.

Hours pass with Blake tossing and turning in bed, his thoughts spiraling in an endless loop. As the night deepens and silence envelops the house, a sense of loneliness creeps into his heart. He feels adrift, lost in a sea of uncertainties and insecurities.

Just as he begins to drift into a fitful slumber, a faint rustling sound catches Blake's attention. He sits up in bed, straining his ears to listen amidst the quiet of the night. The sound repeats, a soft shuffling coming from somewhere outside his window.

Curiosity mingled with unease spurs Blake to get out of bed and approach the window. Slowly drawing back the curtain, he peers into the darkness outside. Moonlight filters through the branches of the trees, casting eerie shadows on the ground below.

And then he sees it — a figure moving stealthily through the shadows, its silhouette barely visible against the night. Blake's heart quickens as he watches, his breath catching in his throat. Who could be prowling around his house at this hour?

Without thinking, he throws on a jacket and quietly slips out of his room, determined to investigate the mysterious presence outside. Each step he takes is cautious, his senses alert to every floor creak. When he reaches the front door, he grips the doorknob and freezes.

"What am I going to do? Am I going to actually confront whoever is lurking in my yard? I've never been in a fight in my life. What if they have a knife or a gun?"

Despite the fear coursing through him, a boost of adrenaline propels Blake forward. Steeling his nerves, he slowly turns the doorknob and steps outside, the cool night air sending a shiver down his spine. He scans the darkness, searching for any sign of movement.

As he moves farther from the safety of his home, the tension in his muscles coils tighter with each passing moment. The figure is now just a few feet away, its outline becoming clearer in the moonlight. Blake's heart pounds in his chest as he prepares himself for whatever confrontation may come.

"Hey! Who's there?" Blake calls out, his voice trembling slightly despite his best efforts to sound firm.

The figure freezes, turning towards him with a sudden jerk of movement. In the dim light, Blake can make out the silhouette of a person. A thud startles him as the figure drops something on the ground and sprints in the opposite direction. Adrenaline surges through his veins as he contemplates chasing after them but decides against it. Instead, he cautiously approaches the abandoned object. Every step seems like an hour as he scans his surroundings, anticipating the figure's return—his heart pounds in his chest, ready for any sudden danger that may come his way.

Bending down to examine the objects left behind, Blake's breath catches in his throat when he sees what it is.

Spray paint. This nightcrawler was going to vandalize his family home.

Blake's mind races with a mix of relief and anger at the realization of the intruder's intentions. The spray paint canisters lie innocuously on the ground, their caps removed and a threatening hiss escaping from the nozzle of one of them. The moonlight casts an eerie glow on the metallic surfaces.

The initial rush of adrenaline slowly subsides, leaving Blake uneasy. His mind is spinning with unanswered questions—who was that? Why his home? Was it simply an act of random vandalism, or was there an actual motive behind it?

Blake picks up the spray paint canisters, his fingers trembling slightly as he examines them in the moonlight. The hissing sound grows louder, a stark reminder of the near miss they just had. His heart still racing, he quickly makes his way back inside, locking the door behind him.

His thoughts are interrupted by the sound of footsteps coming from the hallway. His parents emerge from their room; concern etched on their faces as they take in Blake's disheveled appearance.

"Blake, what's going on?" his father asks, a furrow forming between his brows as he looks at the spray paint his son is holding. "Son? What are you doing?"

Blake hesitates, unsure of where to even begin. He holds up the spray paint canisters, his voice barely above a whisper. "There was someone outside…"

"Ugh, those damn teenagers again!" his father grumbles, obvious anger in his voice. His father lets out a frustrated sigh, running a hand through his hair. "These troublemakers have no respect for other people's property," his father mutters, striding towards the front door. Without hesitation, he swings it open and steps outside, scanning the darkness for any sign of the intruder.

His father's voice cuts through the silence, sharp and commanding. "Who's out there? Show yourself!"

There is no response, only the rustling of leaves in the wind. Slamming the door closed, he snatches the canisters from Blake's hands and drops them into the trash can.

"Alright, well, it looks like you scared the little hoodlum off. I doubt they will be back tonight. I wonder if they hit anyone else's house before they showed up here? Those cans weren't full, so I'm guessing they did."

"You think it was just a random kid?"

"Oh, I'm sure of it. Happens all the time. Kids will be kids, I suppose; I sure wish they were using shaving cream or toilet paper, though. A lot easier to clean up."

"Alright, well, that's enough adventure for one night. Let's all go back to bed and try and get some rest," his mother requests.

After bidding his parents goodnight and closing his bedroom door behind him, Blake collapses onto his bed, the events of the day and now the night replaying in his mind like a broken record. Sleep continues to elude him as he stares at the ceiling, his thoughts consumed by unanswered questions and lingering unease.

Hours pass with Blake tossing and turning in bed, his mind unable to find peace. Every creak of the house sends a jolt of adrenaline through him, his senses on high alert for any sign of danger. Finally, exhaustion takes over his senses, and he falls asleep, only to dream about the retreat and all the scenarios Blake has made up in his head that could go wrong.

The following morning, sunlight filters in through the curtains, casting a warm glow across Blake's room. He awakens groggily, his body still weary from the restless night before. As he sits up in bed, dread fills him as he contemplates the excited chatter he will have to endure from his co-workers, who are eager to go to Blackfoot Wilderness in just a few short days.

He reluctantly gets ready for the day and heads to the office. When he arrives, his interactions with his co-workers only serve to highlight his growing sense of isolation and unease. The day passes by quickly, and before he knows it, Blake is already on his way home.

In the days leading up to the trip, he tries to focus on burying himself in projects and deadlines to distract himself from the impending social challenges he will face. However, no amount of work can silence the anxious thoughts swirling in his mind.

Finally, Friday arrives, and the team gathers in the parking lot, ready to embark on their adventure. As they load onto the rental bus, he finds himself a secluded seat in the back corner, hoping to remain unnoticed throughout the journey. The scenic drive towards Blackfoot Wilderness Campground does little to ease his anxious mind. Instead, he lets his thoughts drift away and get dark. He catches himself several times smirking at the sinister notions of turmoil, misery, and harm coming to his co-workers on this trip.

The drive is filled with laughter and lively conversation, but Blake stays silent, lost in his ruminations. Blake is instantly uncomfortable and out of his element when they arrive and begin setting up camp. They are greeted with breathtaking views of towering pine trees and a serene lake glittering in the sunlight. The air is crisp and fresh, starkly contrasting to the stuffy office atmosphere they left behind.

Despite the picturesque surroundings, Blake's heart pounds with anxiety as he watches his coworkers enthusiastically pitching tents and organizing camp supplies. He fumbles with the tent poles, his hands shaking nervously, while his colleagues set up their accommodations effortlessly. The sound of laughter and camaraderie fills the air, a stark reminder of his own solitude in the midst of the lively group.

Increasingly isolated, Blake excuses himself under the guise of gathering firewood. As he wanders through the forest, his footsteps muffled by the thick carpet of pine needles, he can't shake the anxiety that has settled in his chest like a heavy stone.

Lost in his thoughts, Blake stumbles upon a secluded clearing bathed in dappled sunlight filtering through the trees. A sense of calm washes over him as he sits on a moss-covered rock, enveloped by the soothing sounds of nature. A sense of calmness overtakes him as he sits there, breathing in the earthy scents of pine and damp soil. He finds a moment of peace, a fleeting escape from his thoughts and self-doubt. The experience is unfamiliar, enveloping him like a warm hug. As he relishes the moment, he hears a rustling behind him.

"Please, go away," he whispers. "I'm enjoying the moment of peace."

"We are all gathering together to work on something together."

Blake jumps when he realizes who is behind him. "Mr. Hayes, I'm... I'm sorry... I didn't know it was you. Of course, I..."

"Relax, son. I understand this weekend pushes your boundaries and takes you out of your comfort zone. But I really think that if you just put yourself out there, it will benefit you both professionally and personally. This trip is about trying new things and bonding as a team. And between you and me, the board, CEO, and myself are looking for someone who not only does great work but can also lead, which involves working with your co-workers. Get comfortable in the uncomfortable; if that doesn't work, just fake it. I'm rooting for you, Blake. Don't let me down."

"I know; I'll do my best, sir."

"That's all any of us can do. Come on, let's get back to the group. We are getting started in just a few minutes."

The duo walks back to the campsite together in silence. Blake continues to look behind him, drawn to the clearing. It's as if he is leaving something special behind.

"You good, Blake?" Mr. Hayes questions as he turns to glance in the direction Blake keeps staring.

"Yeah, sorry," he replies, shaking his head and clearing his thoughts.

As the day progresses, Blake tentatively participates in the team-building activities. He discovers that he actually has a knack for problem-solving and surprises his colleagues with some of his creative ideas. Slowly but surely, the barriers between him and the rest of the team start to crumble as they bond over shared experiences and laughter.

By the time evening falls and the team gathers around a crackling campfire, Blake observes he's no longer being treated as if he's the office outcast. He's sharing jokes and stories with his coworkers, relishing in a sense of belonging that he's never experienced before. As they roast marshmallows and gaze up at the starlit sky, Blake realizes that maybe, just maybe, he had been his own worst enemy this entire time. The others seem to be enjoying his company and conversing with him happily.

"Is this really happening?" He wonders.

It was a moment of realization for Blake as if a fog had lifted from his vision. He watches the flickering flames of the campfire dance and cast shadows on the faces of his coworkers. Their smiles seem genuine, and their laughter is infectious. For the first time in what seems like forever, he doesn't feel like an outsider looking in.

As they share stories and bond over the fire, Blake detects a warmth in his chest that has nothing to do with the fire's heat. It's the warmth of acceptance and friendship slowly blooming in the most unexpected places – the Blackfoot Wilderness Campground. "Mr. Hayes was right," he thinks to himself.

With each passing moment, he opens up more, sharing snippets of his life and experiences with his coworkers.

Blake notices that Taylor is staring at him intently and then realizes that she has been making eyes at him for the last hour or two. Taylor is the most beautiful woman Blake has ever seen. He's had a massive crush on her since she was hired last year. However, he knows that he is nowhere near her league. Every guy he's ever known her to date has been tall, muscular, and exceptionally good-looking. Which only makes sense, as she could be a supermodel herself. Her long blonde hair shimmers against the glow of the fire. However, as he glances over again to look at her, he notices she's looking back at him with a welcoming smile. His heart skips a beat as he watches Taylor lean over and whisper something to Christina, her office best friend. They both start laughing and smile over at Blake.

Something about the interaction doesn't sit well in the pit of his stomach, but after having such a good day and finally making so much progress with the rest of the team, he doesn't want to spend too much time overthinking and ruin the rest of the night.

Matt sits down next to Blake on the oversized log and slaps him on the back.

"Hey there, Blake! You really came out of your shell today," Matt exclaims, his boisterous laughter echoing around the campfire.

Blake can't help but smile at Matt's friendly gesture. For once, he's not the outcast watching from the fringes. The fire's warmth, his coworkers' camaraderie, and his newfound sense of acceptance make him perceive he finally belongs.

"Well, that's what this weekend is about, right?" Blake offers sheepishly.

Matt's grin and awkward shrug don't quite mask the smug satisfaction in his voice as he announces, "I guess I'll be taking that promotion from you. I want to be sorry for having to do it to you, but I can't." His laughter is hollow, and an uncomfortable tension settles between them.

"Taking it from me?" Blake questions, instantly annoyed.

"Oh, oh, for fucks sake. Blake, you don't actually think that you're going to get it over me, do you? The presentation is just a formality."

Blake stares back in surprise, unsure what to say. The night has been going so well. Matt has been drinking; perhaps he was overthinking his confident stance.

"I work very hard," Blake finally replies sheepishly.

"We all know you do. Honestly, that's all you seem to do. But that isn't the only thing a senior marketing manager does, dude. You gotta be personable with the clients, too. I'm not trying to be an asshole, man. I'm just saying. Let's be realistic here. That isn't you, and the promotion is mine."

"I guess we'll see," Blake replies snarkily.

"Sure, buddy, may the best man win. Hey, you want a beer?" Matt asks as he places a hand on Blake's shoulder.

"No, I'm good," Blake replies as he scans all of his coworkers as they laugh around the fire. They all seem genuinely happy. Christine is slinking by, ever so close to the roaring flames, and Blake has another sinister thought. He cocks his head to the side and begins to imagine the scenario as it plays through his mind.

Christine sways unsteadily on her feet, a slight flush on her cheeks. She attempts to walk seductively, but it's clear that she's more tipsy than alluring. In her clumsy state, she misses her step and stumbles into the edge of the crackling fire, yelping in pain as her foot makes contact with the flames. Her screams echo throughout the surrounding area, causing everyone to scurry towards her in concern. The once lively atmosphere falls silent as everyone's attention turns to Christine. Amidst the worried murmurs, Blake can't contain his amusement and lets out a burst of laughter, shattering the silence. His companions look at him in disbelief and disgust.

"Dude, seriously. What the fuck?" Axel questions, drawing Blake out of his sinister laughter.

Blake shakes his head and shrugs Axel off.

"I'm sorry, it's just a weird defense mechanism," Blake replies.

Axel raises an eyebrow, his expression skeptical.

Blake shifts uncomfortably on the log, his mind still lingering on the disturbing moment he had just seconds ago. Axel shakes his head and walks away.

As the night progresses, more stories are shared, more laughter fills the air, and Blake finds himself to be happier than he's been in years. The weight of loneliness that had been dragging him down begins to lift, replaced by a newfound sense of connection with those around him.

Taylor keeps shooting him subtle glances and smiling from across the fire, her eyes sparkling with mischief. Blake's heart flutters at the attention his crush is offering.

When she slowly begins making her way toward him, Blake almost pees his pants.

"What is she doing?" he whispers and holds his breath, carefully watching her every move. When she sits down next to him, she's so close that their thighs touch, and electricity pulsates through his entire body until it reaches his manhood. Blake shifts uncomfortably, trying to adjust his ever-growing member before Taylor sees what she's doing to him.

Taylor leans in so close to Blake that her breath is on his cheek. Her lips are just mere inches from his ear. "Do you want to take a walk with me?" she questions softly, sending shivers down his spine.

Blake's heart races with an equal mixture of excitement and apprehension. Taylor stands up gracefully and, without waiting for his response, extends her hand to him. "Come on," she urges.

With a rush of adrenaline, Blake takes her hand, his palms sweaty. As they leave the warmth of the campfire behind and venture into the darkened woods, a sense of adventure surges through him. The moonlight filters through the trees, casting eerie shadows on the forest floor as they silently walk.

Taylor stops, turning to face Blake with a mischievous wink.

2
CHAPTER TWO

As Blake follows Taylor into the darkness of the woods, his heart pounds in his chest with a mixture of anxiety and excitement. The trees loom overhead, casting eerie shadows that seem to dance along the forest floor. He can barely distinguish Taylor's figure ahead of him, her blonde hair a shimmering beacon in the dim light.

They walk silently for a while, the only sound being the crunch of twigs beneath their feet. Blake glances at Taylor, trying to read her expression in the darkness. Finally, she stops and turns to face him.

"Blake, do you want to play a game with me?" she asks, her voice barely above a whisper. Blake's heart pounds in his chest, unsure what to expect from the enigmatic Taylor. But her playful smile is infectious, and he nods in agreement.

"What kind of game?" he manages to ask, his voice betraying a mix of curiosity and nervousness.

Taylor's laughter rings out melodically in the still night air. "A trust game," she answers mysteriously.

Before he can respond, she steps closer and places a blindfold in his hands. "Put this on," she instructs.

Blake hesitates momentarily, his mind racing with a thousand thoughts and uncertainties. But something in Taylor's demeanor puts him at ease, coaxing him to take the leap of faith.

Blake hesitantly ties the blindfold around his head in both excitement and trepidation. As he stands in the darkness, he listens to the sounds of the night surrounding him—the rustle of leaves, the chirping of crickets, and Taylor's soft footsteps as she moves around him.

"Trust me," her voice whispers close to his ear, sending a shiver down his spine. Blake takes a deep breath, pushing aside his inner doubts and fears. He focuses on the sound of Taylor's voice, letting it guide him through this mysterious game.

Her warm and reassuring hand is in his. She leads him forward, each step filled with anticipation. Blake's other senses heighten in the absence of sight—the earthy scent of the forest, the gentle breeze on his skin, and the distant hoot of an owl.

Taylor's touch sends a thrill through him, igniting a sense of wonder and exhilaration. A rush of emotions swirls inside him. Could this be real? Could Taylor honestly be interested in him? Where are we going? What are we doing?" he questions curiously.

"Blake, I've been watching you lately. You have a quiet strength about you that's intriguing. Then today, seeing you open up and connect with everyone, I realize there's so much more to you than I realized."

Blake is dumbfounded. This gorgeous woman is saying things he never thought he'd hear from anyone, let alone her. He takes a deep breath, trying to steady his racing heart. "I... I don't know what to say to that," he admits.

Taylor reaches out and gently places a hand on his arm. The touch sends shivers down Blake's spine. "I know we haven't really talked before, but something about you is drawing me in."

Blake's mind races with a whirlwind of thoughts and emotions. Could this be a trick? A cruel joke orchestrated by his coworkers? Or was Taylor genuinely interested in him, the quiet and reserved Blake who has always felt invisible in a crowd?

Before he can gather his thoughts and respond, Taylor takes a step closer, her face inches away from his. The warmth of her breath against his skin sends a jolt of electricity through his entire being. Blake's heart pounds in his chest as a gush of desire mixed with uncertainty courses through him. She reaches up and unties the blindfold, letting it drop around his neck loosely until it eventually falls to the ground without a sound.

Taylor looks deep into his soul, her gaze unwavering. "I want to get to know the real you, Blake."

Blake is torn between caution and longing. Could he dare to believe that someone like Taylor could see something in him worth pursuing? The doubts and insecurities that have haunted him for so long threaten to resurface, but a glimmer of hope flickers within him.

Summoning his courage, Blake takes a deep breath and meets Taylor's gaze with newfound determination. "I... I would like that," he finally says, his voice barely above a whisper.

The corners of her lips curl as she seductively trails her hands along his thin arms.

Staring down at her five-foot-five frame curiously, he wonders where this will go.

"Take off your clothes, Blake."

"WHAT?" he shrieks.

Taylor chuckles at his shocked response and expression. She dances around him in mischief. "Come on, don't be a big baby," she giggles back playfully.

As he hesitates, Taylor steps closer to him, her gaze locked in on his. "Trust me," she whispers, her hand reaching for the hem of his shirt.

Blake's heart races as he processes Taylor's unexpected request.

In a moment of impulsiveness, he smirks back at her. "I will if you will," he replies nervously.

Taylor's laughter rings out, a melodic sound reverberating in this stillness. Her eyes sparkle with amusement as she considers Blake's cheeky response.

"Ohhh aren't you naughty? Well, that's only fair," she replies. "Okay, here's the deal: I'll go over behind that tree and take off mine, and you stay over here. When you're undressed, toss your clothes by that tree stump, and I'll do the same."

Once again, everything in his rational thinking brain was screaming to return to the campfire with everyone else and not take his clothes off. However, looking at the desire she's displaying at the moment, he senses he's too far in to turn back now and smiles back with a nod.

As he watches her strut a few feet away and hide behind a tree, he begins to take off his shirt. As he removes each piece of clothing, he tosses them onto the nearby stump. It's too dark to see the stump clearly, so he can't tell if all of Taylor's clothing has landed yet.

"Are you ready?" he calls out into the darkness.

A soft rustling of leaves is the only response to Blake's question, the darkness of the woods swallowing up his words.

He stands there, bare and vulnerable, the cool night air caressing his skin as he waits for Taylor's reply. Doubt begins to creep into his mind, a nagging voice questioning the sanity of their impulsive decision.

Just as he starts to regret his choice and consider calling out for Taylor again, a low chuckle breaks through the silence. "Almost there, Blake. Just one more minute," her voice carries through the darkness, filled with a hint of mischief.

Blake's heart pounds in his chest as he strains to catch a glimpse of her figure behind the tree. The seconds pass like an eternity as anticipation builds within him, mingling with nervous energy. Finally, he sees shadowy movement, and then Taylor emerges from behind the tree, fully dressed and holding his clothing in her arms.

"What are you doing?" he shouts in horror.

Only then does he realize that the majority of his other co-workers have gathered behind her to mock and make fun of him, too.

Laughter erupts from the group of co-workers as Blake stands frozen in shock and embarrassment. His face burns with humiliation as he tries to cover himself, his mind racing with a mix of anger and betrayal. Taylor's smirk sends a pang of hurt through him, realizing she had played him for a fool.

The cruel laughter of his colleagues fills the night air, echoing through the stillness of the forest. Blake's heart sinks as he realizes he has been the butt of a humiliating prank orchestrated by Taylor and the others—anger and betrayal rise within him, mixing with deep-seated embarrassment and shame.

His mind whirls with a tumult of emotions—anger at being deceived, pain at being ridiculed, and a deep sense of disappointment in someone he had begun to trust. The darkness around him seems to close in, suffocating him as he struggles to process the betrayal.

As the realization sinks in, Blake looks around at his colleagues' smirking faces, a deep sense of shame washing over him. He wants nothing more than to disappear into the darkness of the forest and never show his face again.

3

CHAPTER THREE

Taylor throws her head back with laughter, the sound echoing through the forest. Blake's heart sinks at the betrayal, realizing he has fallen for a cruel prank. Humiliation washes over him in waves as his coworkers taunt and jeer at his expense.

Exposed and vulnerable, Blake quickly reaches for his clothes, his face burning with shame. The once inviting woods now seem more like a prison, trapping him in this moment of humiliation. Anger simmers beneath the surface as he clenches his fists, struggling to hold back the flood of emotions threatening to consume him.

Taylor saunters closer, a smug smile playing on her lips. "Did you honestly think someone like me would be interested in a loser like you, Blake?" Her words cut through him like a knife, each syllable dripping disdainfully.

Blake's hands tremble, filled with fury and embarrassment, as he faces the harsh reality of the situation—his mind races with thoughts of how to escape this horrifying trap his coworker has set for him. The once-alluring glow in Taylor's seductive look is now a cruel taunt.

With his clothes in hand, he takes off running—away from the group, away from the pain, away from the taunting. After he runs for a few minutes, he stops to put his clothing back on and takes a breath.

"How could I be so stupid?" he berates himself. "There's no way I am going back there tonight."

With a mix of anger, humiliation, and hurt, Blake ventures deeper into the woods, away from the campfire and his coworkers' cruel laughter. The darkness envelops him like a comforting shroud, offering solace from the harsh reality he has just faced. Each step he takes is fueled by a desire to escape, to distance himself from the betrayal that still stings fresh in his heart. The further he wanders, the more the sounds of his coworkers' laughter fade into the distance.

As he continues into the shadowy embrace of the trees, the sounds of the forest envelop him—the rustling of leaves, the distant hoot of an owl, and the gentle trickling of a nearby stream. Nature's symphony is a welcome change from the ridicule and mockery in his memory from a few short moments ago.

Lost in his thoughts, Blake wanders aimlessly through the woods, letting his feet guide him away from the painful memories that linger behind. The cool night air soothes his heated skin, calming the storm of emotions raging within him. He curses himself for falling for such a cruel trick, for letting himself believe even for a moment that someone like Taylor could be genuinely interested in the likes of him.

As Blake stands in the darkness, the noises of the forest engulfing him, he realizes that he's lost and lost not just in the woods but in his own thoughts and emotions. The betrayal stings deeply, cutting through his already fragile sense of self-worth.

With a heavy heart and weary steps, Blake wanders deeper into the woods, trying to put as much distance between himself and the campfire as possible.

His body is beginning to become weary, and he knows he needs to find a safe place to rest and stop for the night. He needs time to figure out what he will do and say when he gets back to camp tomorrow. How is he going to face anyone again? But he has to return to the camp eventually; all his stuff is there, including his phone. They all came together on a bus, driving several hours to get to this campground. An instinctive pull has him turning toward the right in an area he is completely lost in. It's almost as if an invisible string is leading him somewhere. He's too tired to fight it and hopes it will lead him somewhere to rest.

After walking for a few more minutes, the area seems oddly familiar, as if he's in a familiar place. Then the realization hits him. "This is where I was earlier today." The moon hangs above like a silver coin in the velvet sky, casting its ethereal glow over the landscape. Blake is drawn to the small clearing bathed in moonlight, where a carpet of soft grass beckons him to rest. Collapsing onto the ground, he gazes up at the stars twinkling above, a sense of peace washing over him.

In the stillness of the night, surrounded by the gentle whispers of nature, Blake allows himself to breathe, to let go of the hurt and anger that had threatened to consume him. The woods offer him sanctuary, a refuge from the harsh realities of his life and the cruelty of others.

As he lies there under the moon's watchful gaze, he raises his arms and places them underneath his head, looking up toward the sky beyond the treetops.

"Why is this my life?" he asks, letting out an exasperated

sigh. He shifts his arms to try to get a bit more comfortable. However, when he does, something rubs underneath his left arm, and he reaches for it.

It is an oddly shaped stone with a mix of colors he's never seen before. Blake sits up slowly and begins to examine it closely. He's drawn to it, connected somehow and can't stop looking at its unique features. It looks as if it's split perfectly in half.

As Blake turns the stone over in his hands, he notices intricate carvings on its surface that seem to shimmer in the pale moonlight. The stone is warm to the touch and has a melodic hum radiating mysterious energy and pulsating gently as if whispering secrets only he can hear. Mesmerized by its beauty, a sense of calm washes over him.

He lays back down, holding the stone above him, as a shooting star streaks across the night sky, casting a brief but brilliant light on the clearing. Blake's breath catches in his throat, the stone glowing softly in response to the fleeting celestial display. It's as if the universe itself is acknowledging his presence, offering a glimmer of hope in his darkest moment.

As he gazes at the mysterious artifact, a soft and soothing gentle humming fills the air around him, as if the stone itself is singing him a lullaby, wrapping him in a cocoon of tranquility. Blake's eyelids grow heavy, and his mind drifts into a state of peaceful calm.

Blake feels a shift in the air around him in the hazy state between wakefulness and sleep. The gentle hum of the stone seems to grow stronger, vibrating through his very being. Colors begin to dance, swirling and merging in a hypnotic display.

"I wish I was home and no one ever remembered what happened on this stupid trip," he whispers into the night before placing the stone in his right pocket and succumbing to a deep sleep.

The sun radiates on his face long before he opens his eyes. The memories from the night before come flooding back, and he groans. He tosses his arm across his face to block the sun and bids a few extra minutes of denial, unwilling to face the day. The events of last night weigh heavy on him, the sting of betrayal still fresh in his mind. Slowly, he sits up and rubs his face, trying to shake off the memories.

However, when he looks around to survey his surroundings, expecting to be lying in the middle of the woods, he is shocked and confused to find that he is not where he remembers being last night. He is, in fact, in his bed at home. Flinging the blanket off the bed in a panic, he looks down at his clothes and realizes he's still wearing the clothes from last night.

Blake instantly begins playing scenarios through his head about how he got back home and into his bed. His cell phone didn't work in the woods, so he didn't call anyone. Mr. Hayes? No.

"I only had half of one beer; I was barely even drinking; how can I not remember what happened last night?" Frustrated and confused, he searches his memory for any clue that might explain this mysterious turn of events. But the more he tries to piece together the night, the more elusive the memories become.

Blake jumps from the bed and begins pacing back and forth, desperately trying to form a logical explanation.

"It was just a dream? That has to be it. A nightmare, really." He rationalizes.

"Blake, are you ready? If you don't get going soon, you'll be late for work!" He hears his mother call down to him from the top of the stairs.

Thoughts are swirling rapid fire in his head. He reaches for his phone to confirm the date and is flabbergasted to see Monday's displayed on the home screen. "What in the world? Yesterday was Friday; how did I lose two whole days? How did I even get home? When did I get home? Why can't I remember? Was I drugged? Is this another horrible prank by Taylor and whoever else from the office?"

He stumbles into the bathroom, paying very little attention to what he's doing. He can't clear his head enough to gather rational thoughts. With a turn of the knob, the water in the shower races to life. He begins to peel off his clothes, one layer at a time. As his pants hit the floor, a loud thud echoes through the bathroom, and his breath catches in his chest. He looks down to his feet, where he sees the stone tumbled from his pants pocket. He bends down to pick it up. Its warmth against his cool palm causes memories to flood his mind. "Well, that answers one question, unfortunately, I suppose. The trip was real; It wasn't a dream." He murmurs in anguish.

He stands in the bathroom, the stone heavy in his hand, the memories of the night before flooding back with startling clarity. The betrayal, humiliation, and the strange sense of calm he had felt in the woods all felt too real to be just a dream. Blake's mind races with a million questions, his heart pounding in his chest. How could he have brought back a stone from a dream? And what did it signify? Was it a talisman of some sort, a message from the universe? How did he get back home? How did he lose two days? What is going on?

With trembling hands, he sets the stone on the bathroom counter and finishes showering, his thoughts consumed by the mysterious object. As he dresses for work, he can't shake the question that the stone holds some significance, a connection to something beyond his understanding.

Blake decides to keep the stone with him, slipping it into his pocket as he heads up the stairs, his mind on overdrive.

4

CHAPTER FOUR

When he reaches the top of his stairs, he finds his mother standing there looking concerned.

"I was just about to call back down for you. You're going to be late son. Oh, my. Are you okay? You don't look very good. Are you sick? Here, let me check you." His mother places her hand against his forehead with a look of genuine concern on her face. "Don't seem like you have a fever, but you look like you've seen a ghost. What's wrong?"

Blake's face contorts into a strained smile as he looks at his mother, desperately trying to hide the inner turmoil consuming him. "It was just a nightmare, Mom. I'll be okay," he reassures her, though his voice betrays him, and the words sound like lies.

His mother's concerned gaze lingers on him, and he can't help but feel guilty for hiding the truth from her. But how could he possibly explain the confusing jumble of experiences and thoughts that are plaguing him? How could he burden her with his problems when she already has so much on her plate?

He can figure this out on his own without stressing out his already stressed parents.

His mother studies him momentarily, filled with maternal worry. "If you ever need to talk about anything, I'm here for you, sweetheart."

Blake forces a smile, grateful for his mother. "I know, Mom, thanks."

As he prepares to head out for work, the events of the night before continue to haunt him, gnawing at his self-confidence and trust in others. Despite his efforts to push aside the lingering doubts and humiliation, he realizes he has to walk into the office and face his coworkers, the same ones who had just the day before humiliated and mentally tortured him. But it wasn't the day before; it was days before. How can he be missing an entire weekend? "Drugged," he murmurs to himself. That makes so much more sense. Of course, he was drugged; that's why he can't remember what happened. "Fucking Taylor and the other idiots from the office," he seethes. The more he thinks about it, the angrier he gets. "So who knows what else happened, what other awful things they may have done, or what I may have done!" That thought sends shivers down his spine. The idea that he may have made a greater fool out of himself than what he remembers is almost terrifying.

"The office atmosphere is going to be straight torture."

The mere thought of walking in this morning is suffocating, making it hard for him to take a deep breath. He's trapped, caught between the fear of returning and the urge to quit and find another job. Each passing moment brings a new wave of uncertainty and distress, leaving him unsure if he can handle it. But then the anger sets in, knowing he shouldn't have to run away from a toxic environment. He didn't do anything wrong. He takes a deep breath and tries to steady his nerves, determined to stay away and ignore anyone who attempts to bother him today. After all, an important new client is coming in today. Hopefully, everyone will be too busy with their campaign to give him a second glance. Once he gets this promotion, he can deal with his co-workers.

As he exits the house and steps into the bright morning sunlight, a wave of dizziness washes over him, almost causing him to stumble. Instinctively, he grips the stone in his pocket, takes a deep breath, and steadies himself. The world around him seems to shimmer momentarily, as if reality itself is in flux.

Ignoring the disorienting sensation, Blake reaches for his bike and heads for the office.

The morning air is cool against his skin as he pedals through the familiar streets, the rhythmic motion helping to clear his mind. The city begins to wake up around him, a cacophony of honking cars and bustling pedestrians filling the air. But amidst the chaos, Blake feels a strange sense of detachment, as if he's moving through a world that no longer entirely belongs to him.

Arriving at the office building downtown, he chains his bike to a nearby post instead of the usual bike rack in the garage to avoid seeing anyone. He takes a moment to compose himself before stepping inside. The lobby is bustling with activity, colleagues filing past with cups of coffee in hand and phones pressed to their ears. Blake tries to blend into the sea of faces, avoiding any type of contact and quickening his pace towards his office.

As he settles into his chair, the thought of facing his coworkers, those who had betrayed him in one way or another, fills him with dread. But as he sits at his desk and opens his laptop, a strange sense of calm washes over him. The stone in his pocket seems to hum softly, its energy enveloping him in a protective cocoon.

Taking a deep breath, he begins to sift through his emails and prepare for the day ahead. The usual chatter and gossip around the office seem muffled and distant, as if he's viewing them through a haze. Colleagues pass by his cubicle without giving him a second glance, their attention diverted elsewhere.

As the morning progresses, Blake is immersed in his work like never before. Ideas flow effortlessly from his mind, and his fingers fly across the keyboard with precision and speed. Each task is completed with a sense of ease and confidence that surprises even him. Hours pass without him even realizing it. The only thing that brought him out of his groove was the thunderous sound of heavy footsteps echoing down the hall, sending a surge of fear through him.

He immediately identifies the footsteps as belonging to Axel, one of the most notorious bullies in the office. Axel is known for his intimidating presence and cruel treatment of Blake. He always seems to be laughing and joking with everyone else, but when it comes to Blake, he makes it his mission to make his life a living hell. As his heart starts racing, he prepares for another unpleasant encounter. After the embarrassing incident at the retreat, he can't even begin to imagine how this one will go.

Blake takes a deep breath, preparing for whatever confrontation Axel may bring.

"Well, well, well. It's interesting to see you hiding in your office instead of joining us in the conference room," Axel sneers maliciously. "Can't handle being around others, can you?"

Blake squares his shoulders, refusing to show any sign of weakness in front of Axel. "I prefer working in a quieter envi-ronment where I can focus better. Nothing personal," he responds calmly, though inside, he is seething with anger at Axel's taunts. The tension between them crackles in the air, both men sizing each other up like predators circling their prey.

Axel leans in closer, his breath reeking of coffee and arrogance. "You know, Blake, you really should learn to lighten up. Maybe then people wouldn't find you so... unpleasant to be around," he says, clearly enjoying getting under Blake's skin.

But instead of rising to the bait, Blake surprises himself by chuckling softly. "I've been told my resting face is intimidating. I'll work on my smile," he replies with a shrug and a faint glimmer of amusement.

Axel's smirk falters, caught off guard by Blake's unexpected response. He's clearly not used to Blake standing up to him or deflecting his insults so effortlessly. A dangerous scowl crosses Axel's features as he leans in even closer, his voice dropping to a low, menacing whisper.

"You think you're clever, don't you?" Axel sneers, his tone dripping with malice. "But we both know the truth, don't we? You're nothing but a coward hiding behind your desk, too scared to face the reality of who you really are."

Blake meets Axel's gaze head-on, his jaw set in determination. "And who am I, exactly?" he challenges, his voice steady despite the adrenaline and fear coursing through his veins.

"You're a nobody, Blake. Just a pathetic excuse for an employee," Axel spits out, his words like venom.

Blake grits his teeth as Axel's insults hit him like a slap. Despite the provocation, he clenches his fists under his desk, trying to hold onto his composure. In one hand, he grips a small stone tightly, channeling his unease into strength and anger. His usual reserved demeanor has disappeared, replaced by a newfound boldness that urges him to confront the man twice his size in front of him.

"What the hell do you want, Axel? Can't you see I'm busy?"

Axel smirks, malice written all over his face. "Mr. Hayes sent me to find you."

"Mr. Hayes sent me to find you," Axel responds with a cocky smirk, clearly enjoying the power dynamic between them.

Blake scoffs, his voice dripping with sarcasm. "Well, isn't that nice? Now you can scurry back like the lackey you are and tell Mr. Hayes that you found me, and I'm perfectly fine."

Axel's smug chuckle echoes through the room. "Looks like someone finally grew a pair." He leans in, tauntingly close to Blake's face. "But it might be too late for that."

"Just get out and leave me alone," Blake snaps.

Axel's voice is laced with steel as he glares at the defiant man before him. "Mr. Hayes gave me explicit instructions to retrieve you for the group meeting this afternoon," he growls, his arms folding tightly against his chest. "You can either come willingly, or I'll drag you there myself." With a determined stride, Axel motions towards the door.

Blake holds back a sigh, fully aware that trying to reason with Axel would only prolong this uncomfortable encounter. With reluctance, he begins to walk towards the conference room, his anxiety increasing with each step. As he turns the corner and catches sight of Taylor and the rest of the team sitting at the table, his breath catches in his throat. He mentally braces himself for any teasing or ridicule that might come his way. "I won't let them get to me," he reminds himself, rubbing the stone in his pocket.

When he enters the room, a heavy silence falls over the space. He takes his usual spot in the back, surrounded by empty seats. As soon as he sits down, they resume their chatter amongst themselves. It's as if he's invisible to everyone else. "How strange," he thinks to himself. "I can't believe no one is saying anything about what happened." His focus darts around the room, searching for any reaction, but all he finds is indifference. Until, he locks gazes with Taylor, and a jolt of anger shoots through him. But to his surprise, she merely looks away, unfazed by his presence. The lack of attention or acknowledgment only adds to his confusion.

As the meeting progresses, a wave of relief washes over him. The energy he had been so powerfully aware of earlier seems to be fading. The protective cocoon is dissipating, leaving him vulnerable to the world around him once more. He focuses on taking notes and staying engaged in the conversation, but his mind keeps drifting back to the confrontation earlier.

The rest of the meeting progresses without any problems, but Blake remains lost in his thoughts, detached from the discussion around him. As the meeting draws to a close and people begin to leave, Blake stays seated, deep in thought. Mr. Hayes notices his distant demeanor and approaches with concern etched on his face, cutting through the post-meeting chatter.

"Blake, are you alright?"

"Yes, sir, I'm just focused on my tasks. Sorry."

"Are you feeling better?" His voice filled with genuine worry. "I had hoped the retreat would bring you closer to your colleagues, but I understand why you couldn't attend. Illness always seems to strike at the worst times."

Blake stares back at him with a neutral expression, trying to conceal his surprise. He shifts his weight nervously between his feet. What does he mean he wasn't at the retreat? Memories come flooding back - the pain, embarrassment ...the regret. He puts his hands in his pockets and brushes up against the stone, realizing what Mr. Hayes meant by "couldn't make it."

5

CHAPTER FIVE

As Mr. Hayes continues to speak, his words become muffled background noise, Blake's heart pounding as he contemplates what he just heard. "Is it possible? Could the stone be the key to all of this? Is that why Mr. Hayes thinks I wasn't there? Why Taylor didn't acknowledge me or say anything about the incident? Or anyone else, for that matter. How? How could this be possible?" More and more questions course through his thoughts.

The stone is warm in his hand, vibrating with an other-worldly energy that sends a shiver down his spine. Blake's mind races as he tries to make sense of the swirling thoughts.

Could the stone be more than just a simple piece of nature? He struggles to believe it, telling himself that these things only happen in fairy tales and movies. But as he holds it in his hand, he can't help but notice a surge of strength that makes him question everything he thought he knew about magic. Could this stone hold some power beyond his understanding, a connection to something mysterious and unknown? He debates with himself, trying to rationalize and dismiss the idea. "It can't be," he insists. "It's not possible."

"Blake, are you even listening to me?" Mr. Hayes demands.

Blake snaps out of his daydream and quickly becomes aware of the reality around him. He rubs his hand across his face in embarrassment. "I apologize, Mr. Hayes. I must have zoned out."

"It's okay, Blake. If you're still not feeling well, you can take the rest of the day off. You won't be any good to me if you're not fully present. You can't even hold a simple conversation-with your boss!"

"No, sir, I'm fine. Really. I'm sorry, it won't happen again. I just have a lot on my mind."

"Listen, as you know, you and Matt are up for this promotion. Whoever gets it will lead our new campaign. But if your head isn't in the game, maybe it's not the right time for you. This decision is too important to be given to someone who isn't fully committed."

"Please, trust me. I truly want this opportunity and am confident that I am the perfect candidate for the job. I may be a bit off today, but I assure you that I can handle it. My vision for the new campaign is clear, and I know exactly how to make it a resounding success."

"Well, you have just one week to finalize your presentation. The decision on who gets the account and promotion will be announced later that day."

Blake's voice pleads as he says, "I'll be ready, sir. I promise." He's been passed over for promotions in the past few years, and he finally asked Mr. Hayes why. Apparently, it's because he doesn't put himself out there enough. Blake knows he'll never win any popularity contests, but that doesn't reflect on his hard work or the quality of his work. Recently, though, Mr.

Hayes has been pushing him to move up, saying he sees potential in him.

His boss studies him carefully before shrugging and saying, "Alright then, but if you need to leave early today, just let me know. Get back to work."

"Yes, of course." Blake scurries back to his office. Once sitting at his desk, he pulls the stone from his pocket and places it carefully on the notepad in front of him. He leans forward, getting within inches of the stone. As he stares at it intently, he swears he can see it vibrating ever so slightly. "Is my mind playing tricks on me? I know that there is no way that this is actually possible. But what other explanation can there be? The only other option is I'm losing my mind."

Blake's gaze remains fixed on the stone, its faint vibrations sending a current of strength through him. The weight of the unknown presses down on his shoulders, each unanswered question fueling his growing sense of disorientation. His rational mind rebels against the notion of supernatural forces at play, yet the evidence before him defies all logical explanations.

With a sudden increase of determination, Blake reaches out to pick up the stone, its warmth seeping into his palm like a living pulse.

Ignoring the nagging doubts that claw at the edges of his consciousness. Blake closes his eyes and takes a deep breath, focusing on the whispered words echoing in his mind.

He can't take the wait any longer. He wants to research and see what he can find about the stone. The office computers are all monitored, and he doesn't want anyone to know what he is looking at, so he grabs his phone and pulls up the internet browser. As he begins typing his query, he is met with a black screen.

"Are you serious?" he grumbles as he presses the button on

the side, knowing it won't turn back on. "I don't even know how or when I got home, so I shouldn't be surprised I didn't charge this stupid thing." He slams the phone onto his desk in frustration and tries to ignore the curious glances of his coworkers overhearing his ridiculous fit.

He makes his way through the day absentmindedly. By the time it's five o'clock, he isn't sure how he got anything done or if he even did. All he can think about is getting information on the stone. He closes up his office and heads for the door, but he is stopped by his office nemesis, Axel.

Axel's sneering face looms in the doorway, blocking Blake's path with an arrogant grin—his taunting words slice through the air like knives, laced with condescension and designed to provoke. "Leaving already, Blake?" he scoffs.

Blake's jaw clenches, his patience worn thin after a day of suppressing his inner turmoil. "I have things to do, Axel. Now move," he responds sharply.

Axel's grin widens at Blake's curt reply, clearly relishing the chance to push his buttons further. "What's the rush? Got a hot date with your hand?" he jeers.

A gush of rage flows through Blake at the insult, but he forces himself to remain calm. "What I'm doing is none of your business, Axel. Now get out of my way," he orders firmly.

Axel chuckles dismissively and steps aside, but not entirely out of the way. "Enjoy dinner with your mommy, loser," he sneers. "Hope she gives you something better than last time so you don't get another tummy ache. That's the real reason why you couldn't come to our retreat, right? Your mommy's cooking made you sick? Don't want you getting food poisoning again now, do we, buddy?"

"I wish you would," Blake mutters under his breath.

"What was that?" Axel demands, getting in Blake's face. "Say it out loud, coward."

Just move," Blake snarls, forcefully pushing past Axel and storming outside.

"Is that all you have to say? Fucking idiot. Grow a pair, dude." Axel's mocking laughter echos off the walls as Blake continues to seeth with anger, fists clenched at his sides.

Blake's body tenses as he refuses to even look at Axel, his hand jolting into the air to thrust his middle finger in Axel's direction. He wrenches his bike out of the rack and mounts it angrily in one swift motion.

As he speeds away, the cold wind whipping past him, Blake can't shake the anger flowing through him. He knows he needs to focus on finding information about the stone, but Axel's taunts linger in his mind, fueling his rage. He allows his mind to shift from his rage toward Axel, instead letting it race with questions about his newfound mysterious object.

As he contemplates his next move, his excitement and curiosity start to build once more. "How can I gather information about this he wonders to himself. I'll probably begin where most people do—with a simple Google search." The sun's warm rays shine down upon him as he makes his way back home, taking in his neighborhood's familiar sights and smells. With each turn of his bike pedals, his determination to unravel the object's secrets grows stronger.

After a long day, his porch was a familiar landing spot, but he didn't bother with his usual routine tonight. Instead of carefully placing his bike against the rail, he haphazardly tossed it aside and sprinted through the front door and down into the basement. With a sense of urgency driving him, he plugged in his phone and tossed it onto the bed before booting up his computer. His fingers flew across the keyboard with lightning speed, scouring through countless web pages, forums, and articles in search of any information that could shed light on the mysterious stone he had found earlier that day. The blue glow of the monitor bathed his face as he delved deeper into the research, consumed by both urgent curiosity and overwhelming intrigue; hours passed in a blur as he lost himself in the wealth of knowledge at his fingertips. Yet, despite all his efforts, none seemed to offer the wisdom he so desperately sought.

He rubs his face in frustration before taking a deep breath. "This is ridiculous. That piece of earth I found in the woods couldn't possibly have some kind of magical power. What's wrong with me?" he scolds himself. As he moves to close the search on his computer, one article catches his attention. He clicks on it and reads through it three times, heart racing. Could it be? As unbelievable as it sounds, the stone he holds in his hand could truly possess such powers. The article speaks of a secret lineage tasked with protecting the stone and its secrets from falling into the wrong hands, hinting at its extraordinary abilities. It references a specific book, 'Ancient Histories of the Earth and the Powers Within,' as its source of information.

"I have to get my hands on this book," he mutters under his breath, frantically typing the title into Amazon's search bar. But to no avail. He tries Google next, and finally finds a listing for an independent bookstore about an hour away. He quickly jots down the phone number and dials it with shaky fingers. The phone rings twice before a voice answers on the other end of the line.

"Hello, Moonlight Books, how can I help you?"

Blake takes a deep breath to steady his nerves. "Hi, I'm looking for a specific book called Ancient Histories of the Earth and the Powers Within. Do you happen to have it in stock?"

The voice on the other end paused before responding, "Interesting book choice. What has you searching for that particular book? It's a rare find and not something many people even know about."

Blake hesitated before answering, "Research purposes. Can you please check if you have it available?"

Growing more frustrated by the second, Blake's patience wears thin as he awaits an answer from the person on the other end of the line. He desperately hoped that they would have the book he needed in stock.

"I'm sorry," the voice on the other end responds with a hint of hesitation in their tone. "That book is nearly impossible to find, and I don't have it in stock. But there may be someone who does. A collector of rare and elusive books. He's known to be quite selective with his sales, but for the right price, he may part with it."

A spark of hope ignites in Blake's chest at the mere mention of finding the coveted book. "Can you please give me his contact information? My research depends on it."

"I cannot simply hand out someone's personal information without their consent," the voice replies firmly. "But I will reach out to my contact and pass along your information. If he decides to speak with you, he will contact you."

"But what if he doesn't reach out to me?" Blake begs.

"If he doesn't contact you, he's not interested in speaking with you. Now, if you give me your information, I can pass it along to him."

Blake quickly rattles off his contact information to the person on the other end of the line, hoping against hope that this mysterious collector would reach out to him. With a sense of anticipation and impatience gnawing at him, he thanks the bookstore employee and hangs up the phone.

Hours pass without a word from the mysterious book collector. Blake tries to focus on his presentation, but his mind keeps drifting back to thoughts of the ancient book and its secrets.

Finally, after the sun has gone down, Blake sits on his bed, lost in thought, when his phone buzzes from the nightstand beside him. His heart leaps into his throat as he looks at the unknown number flashing on the screen; he answers the call.

"Hello?" he says, trying to keep his voice steady and even.

A low, gravelly, cracking voice responded from the other end. "Is this Blake?"

"Yes, speaking." Blake's heart races with excitement.

"I hear you're looking for a particular book. Uhh, let's see. Oh..yes, 'Ancient Histories of uhh....

"Yes, yes, that's correct," Blake interrupts him.

"Welp, you're in luck. I happen to have that very book," the voice continues, each word carefully enunciated. "However, this book is not for everyone. Now, why exactly do you need it? I don't just go about offering my books to just anyone. Why should I let it go to you? ?"

"I...UHHH...I DON'T KNOW," Blake stammers, caught off guard by the question and the tone in which it was asked.

"You don't know? Again, why the hell do you want it? What do you want with the book then?"

"I'm doing research."

"Ahh, research, I see, then perhaps this is not the book for you. Good day."

Blake's voice cracks with desperation as he pleads, "NO! Wait!" The caller hesitates before hanging up, and Blake takes a deep breath to continue. His words tumble out in a frantic, jumbled mess, "I found this stone about a week ago, and it's been consuming my every waking thought. I know it sounds insane, but I think it may be...."

"Special?" the mysterious caller interjects.

"More than that," Blake replies, his voice trembling with excitement and fear. "It's like nothing I've ever seen before."

There is a long pause on the other end of the line before the gravelly voice responds again. "Very well, uhh, meet me at midnight by the old oak tree in the abandoned park on the outskirts of town." The man on the phone hangs up.

Blake's heart pounds with a mixture of anticipation and fear at the thought of meeting the mysterious book collector. Midnight is still hours away, but he cannot focus on anything else. Instead, he paces back and forth in his room, his mind racing. "This is insane. I'm going to meet a random creepy guy alone in an abandoned park at midnight. It's the beginning of every horror movie ever. But what other choice do I have?" he spends the next few hours going back and forth reasoning with himself.

As the moon rises high in the sky and the world around him falls into a deep slumber, Blake slips out of his house, making sure to move silently so as not to wake his parents. The streets are eerily quiet as he pedals his bike towards the abandoned park, the only sound being the gentle hum of insects in the warm night air.

As he arrives at the park, the old oak tree looms in front of him. Its gnarled branches cast strange shadows in the moonlight. As he approaches, a figure steps out from behind its twisted trunk.

Blake takes a step forward, allowing his vision to adjust to the dim light for a minute. "Who are you?" he asks cautiously. A fragile-looking older man with a hunchback walks out into the light. He scrutinizes Blake for a moment before he speaks.

"Show me the stone."

Reluctantly, Blake reaches into his pocket and pulls out the mysterious stone. He holds it tightly in his grip in case the man attempts to take it from him, and he holds it up for the man to see.

"And there it is. Where did you find this?" the older man asked.

"It sort of found me," Blake replies cautiously.

"Yes, that would be the way it would happen, wouldn't it," the man murmurs, gazing at the stone intensely.

"Blake," the mysterious man begins, his voice etching a chill down Blake's spine. "I have the book, but before you're allowed to see it, you must promise to uphold the responsibility that comes with it. The man stops to cough and clears his throat. You must; you must guard its secrets. You hear?"

Blake nods in understanding, a mix of apprehension and curiosity swirling in his mind. The man steps closer and hands him a weathered, leather-bound book with intricate patterns etched into its cover. As Blake flips through its yellowed pages, a strange energy emanates from the text as if the book itself is alive.

"This book contains the histories you seek, the origins of the stone you hold in your hand," the man explains solemnly. "But remember, knowledge comes with a price. The powers within these pages are not to be trifled with. Many take that for granted and regret it later. Don't become one of them."

Blake nods his head absentmindedly, his fingers tracing the cover. "Uh, yeah, sure. Look, I'm not trying to turn into a superhero. I just want to understand the powers of this stone. I think I'll be okay."

The older man shakes his head in disgust and sighs. "You've been warned." And turns to walk away.

"Excuse me, how much do I owe you?"

The older man doesn't turn around but says cryptically, "The book is not mine to sell. It belongs to no one.

"Noted." Blake replies, pulling the book into his chest and turning back toward his bike.

The old man turns around and says, "Heed my words. Pay

close attention. Fully understand what you're getting yourself into."

Blake looks back, stunned, and pauses. After a moment, he shrugs his shoulders and continues walking toward his bike.

With a final nod, the mysterious man disappears into the shadows, leaving Blake alone in the moonlit park with the book in one hand and the stone in the other. A cool breeze stirs the leaves around him, mounts his bike, and makes his way back home.

He sneaks into the house as quietly as he had exited it earlier and silently makes his way downstairs. Entering his room, he flops onto his bed, book in hand. With a deep breath, he opens the book to its first page, the musty scent of aged paper filling his senses. The words on the page seem to shimmer and dance in the faint light.

As Blake delves into the book's first chapter, his mind is immediately consumed by the words on the page. The text weaves a tale of forgotten civilizations, mystical artifacts, and historic prophecies that send shivers down his spine. He reads about the stone he holds in his hand, learning of its true origins and the incredible power it possesses.

Hours pass unnoticed as he immerses himself in the mesmerizing words, each page revealing more mysteries and secrets than he could have ever imagined. The night slips away, replaced by the pale light of dawn filtering through his window, but Blake remains captivated.

Whatever you desire within the parameters laid out before you will be granted. However, as with every choice you make in life, there is a consequence. Blake let out an exasperated sigh at the thought of rules.

But suddenly, his mother's piercing screams shatter the peaceful silence of the night. He throws the book aside in a split second and leaps out of bed. He bolts up the stairs, each step pounding beneath his feet as he races toward the source of his mother's cries. The urgency in her voice sends chills down his spine, erasing any trace of the book from his mind. Bursting into the living room, he skids to a stop and freezes, heart pounding in his chest. The only sound he can hear is the frantic beat of his own pulse as he takes in the devastating scene before him.

6

CHAPTER SIX

His father is sprawled on the tattered, lumpy couch, his ashen face drenched in a cold sweat. His mother is crouched over him; phone pressed to her ear as she frantically pleads with the person on the other end of the line, her tears creating a trail down her cheeks.

Blake's heart plummets at the sight of his father's frail form. He flies to his mother's side as fear and panic accompany him as he tries to grasp the severity of the situation.

"What happened? What's wrong?" Blake's voice cracks with emotion.

His mother's bloodshot eyes meet his, her voice trembling with desperation. "We were just finishing our morning coffee when he collapsed out of nowhere. The ambulance is on its way, but I don't know what else to do..." Her words trail off into a gut-wrenching silence.

Blake glances at his watch, the glowing numbers showing five a.m. He's been up all night reading.

His heart pounds in his chest as he frantically tries to make sense of the chaotic emergency unfolding before him. He falls to his knees beside his father, gripping his shoulder with a trembling hand. "Dad, please, you have to fight through this!" But his words fall on deaf ears as his father remains motionless, unresponsive. Desperate and filled with anguish, Blake murmurs under his breath, "I just wish you were healthy again." ." In an instant, a blinding golden light bursts forth from within him, engulfing the room in its warm glow. The light swirls around Blake, pulsating with a powerful energy before surging towards his father's lifeless body on the couch. As it envelops him, the light seems to breathe new life into his wounded form, filling him with a radiant vitality. The air crackles with electricity, and the room is alight with shimmering golden hues, like a feverish dream coming to life. And amidst it all, Blake stands alone in awe of this miraculous power he holds within him - the ability to manipulate time and heal those he loves.

Blake watches in awe as his father's complexion takes on a healthier hue. The color returns to his cheeks as he stirs with a bewildered expression. His mother gasps in amazement, the phone slipping from her hand, as she watches the miraculous transformation unfold right in front of her.

His father blinks several times, looking around in confusion before his gaze lands on Blake. "What happened?"

Blake hears the sirens in the background as they rush toward his family home to rescue a man who looks perfectly healthy when, just a few seconds ago, he looked as if he was near death.

Blake's heart races as his father struggles to sit up on the couch, confusion etched onto his face. The room is filled with palpable tension, and Blake can't imagine the weight of his mother's worry as she hurries to embrace her husband.

"Thank God you're alright," she sobs, her grip on him tight.

His dad's response was somber as he recounted his recent

pain. "I thought I was about to die. But now I'm fine, better than fine, actually."

Blake let out a sigh of relief. "No one's going to die today," he reassured them.

But their moment of calm was quickly interrupted by a loud pounding on the door. It flies open, and paramedics rush into the room, immediately attending to the patriarch.

Despite his protests that he was better now, they insisted on taking him to the hospital for further examination. "You may have had a heart attack," one of them explained. "The doctors won't know the extent of the damage until we run some tests."

"I understand your concern, but I assure you, I'm completely fine now," his father argues. "In fact, I haven't felt this good in years." Blake watches as the paramedics carefully maneuver his father onto a stretcher and carry him out of the house, hoping for the best but fearing for the worst.

As he stands in the now-silent living room, the golden light from before is now long gone. He slowly makes his way back down to the basement and stops at the foot of his bed. He sees the book sitting where he tossed it after hearing his mother scream, and his breath hitches in his throat. The realization of what just occurred settles into the pit of his stomach, and he sinks onto the bed with a mixture of exhaustion and elation.

He stares at the book on the floor dumbfounded. Allowing the events he just witnessed to whirl through his mind like a tornado. He is left with a sense of disbelief and wonder. Reaching into his pocket, he pulls out the stone, gazing at it intently. "I wished good health for my father. And it happened. It actually happened."

His vision bounces back and forth between the stone and the leather-bound book. "You've got to be kidding me," he mutters, his hand trembling around the object. The power emanating from it is intoxicating. At that moment, he finally understands what the man was trying to tell him last night. This information must not be taken lightly - it must be protected at all costs. If this kind of power fell into the wrong hands...the thought alone sent shivers down Blake's spine.

Taking in his surroundings, he realizes his room is immaculate. It's as if every item has been meticulously placed in its proper spot. With a sense of urgency, Blake starts to panic. He needs to hide this book before anyone else finds out about it. But where? Nothing seems worthy or secure enough for such a precious possession.

After some consideration, Blake settles on a temporary spot until he can come up with a better solution. He rummages through the back of his closet and retrieves an old backpack, dust clinging to its frayed edges. Carefully, he places the book inside and covers it with a dirty shirt, hoping to conceal its true value. With one last glance around the room, he tucks the bag as far back as possible behind other items on the floor. He even goes so far as to pile his shoes in front of it as if creating a barricade. Only then does he breathe out a slight sense of relief, knowing that, for now, his secret remains safe within the confines of the backpack.

$$7$$

CHAPTER SEVEN

Blake's heart pounds in his chest as he anxiously waits for his mother's call. Every minute creeps by slowly like an eternity passing, each second filled with dread and worry. While he knows what he saw in the moment he made the wish for his father, he still finds it hard to believe. He nervously awaits confirmation from the doctors that his dad is healthy. Finally, his phone rings after what seems like hours, and he practically jumps to answer it.

"Mom, what's going on? What did the doctors say?"

"Blake, they...they don't know," his mother's voice is shaky and filled with disbelief. "The doctor said your father's test results are completely baffling. They've ruled out all life-threatening conditions but can't explain what happened. He said that despite all of your father's symptoms this morning, he is in excellent health."

"Oh, thank goodness!" Blake exclaims. "When will you guys be able to come home?"

"The doctor wants to run one more test, but everything

looks good. Your father should be released soon after that. Aunt Cathy is going to pick us up and drive us back."

"That's such a relief, Mom. Are you sure you don't want me to come get you, though? Aunt Cathy doesn't need to drive all that way."

"No, no, it's okay. You have to get to work. We'll be fine."

"I'm not going to work today, Mom. I want to be here when you and Dad get home."

"Son, don't be ridiculous. Your dad is fine. Go to work, and we'll see you when you get home. Plus, you have that important presentation to prepare for your promotion!" His mother reassures him.

"Are you sure? I think like I should be here just in case."

"Trust me, if you could see how lively your dad is right now, you wouldn't be concerned at all!"

"Well, if you're sure, but keep me posted when you get home and how he's doing throughout the day."

"I promise, honey. Oh, the nurse just walked in. I have to go. I love you. Have a good day at work." With that, his mother hangs up the phone.

Blake tosses his phone onto his bed and plops down beside it. The softness of his comforter beneath him as he stares at the cracked paint on the ceiling. He can't shake the images of his father's pale, sweaty face and the sound of his ragged breathing. A lone thought consistently pops into his thoughts- the stone; it obviously performed a miracle based on his simple wish; however, if he hadn't been there to use it, would his father still be alive? He can't bear the thought. At that moment, Blake knows he has the power to change his life and in the best possible way. The same can't be said for anyone who has crossed him, though. A sinister smirk plays at the edges of his lips as he creates sinister scenarios in his mind.

"I can't believe I am not exhausted," Blake thinks as he realizes he needs to get ready for work. "I've been up all night."

He jumps off the bed and heads to the shower, ready to face the day. He places the stone on the counter and cringes as he takes a good look at himself in the mirror. He's never liked his scrawny frame, but no matter how hard he tries, he just can't put on weight. Scrutinizing all of the details about his face and body, he has an idea.

"I wish I was attractive and muscular," he states expectantly. Blake continues to stare at himself confidently, but after a few seconds, nothing happens. He thinks back to the light that emitted around his father this morning and looks all around the room, hoping to see it again. But nothing is happening. He picks up the stone from the counter and shakes it.

"Maybe there is a limit on how many times you can use it within a certain time period or something," he mumbles, entering the steaming hot shower disappointed. He is even more disappointed when he exits the shower and is met with the same body he entered with. "Still nothing."

Drying himself off, Blake can't shake off the disappointment that lingers within him. Was his power limited? Was it a one-time miracle that he was lucky enough to witness? Or perhaps he had little control over how the stone granted wishes if that's genuinely what it did.

He quickly gets dressed, drops the stone into his pocket, and heads toward the stairs. As he passes his full-length mirror, he stops to look at himself again. Squaring up his shoulders, he imagines how different his life would be if he were better looking.

"All I want is to be muscular and handsome. Why is that too much to wish for?"

Instantly, his pocket begins to shake, and the same glow

from earlier begins to dance around him. His vision gets blurry, and he can no longer see clearly. Yanking off his glasses, he looks into the mirror and is surprised to see. Actually, see, without his glasses. And what he sees shocks him to the core.

He's handsome and now has a very athletic frame. Everything he has ever imagined and hoped to look like. All the qualities he had longed to have himself whenever a handsome stranger crossed his path. The chiseled jawline, the toned and muscular body. He now has it all.

Reaching down to the floor, he grabs his glasses and puts them back on, only to find himself looking back at a blurry reflection again.

"Even my eyesight?"

The stone stops pulsing and rests motionless in his pocket. He thinks back to the wish he had made in the bathroom. " That time, it was on the counter, but it was in my pocket this time. It only works if it's on me," he realizes. "That is very good information to know."

Fueled with more confidence than he's ever had, he saunters up the stairs, ready to tackle the day in a whole new way.

"Watch out, world, I've finally arrived."

As Blake steps out of his house, a sense of determination fills him. Today is the day he takes control of his own destiny. He has the power of the ancient stone coursing through him, and it fuels his every step. With newfound confidence, he heads to work.

The office buzzes with the usual energy as Blake walks in. Colleagues nod in greeting, and he can't help but notice a few surprised looks at his newfound sense of self-assurance. Just as he reaches his office, his boss, Mr. Hayes, greets him.

"Good morning, Blake; I'm glad you're here. I just got a call from Axel's girlfriend. He is violently ill. Apparently he got terrible food poisoning last night. He's actually in the hospital right now on an IV, trying to get some fluids back in him. Anyway, he was supposed to be in a meeting this morning presenting a new campaign to one of our clients. I would really appreciate it if you could take over that meeting for him."

"He got food poisoning?" Blake questions slowly. The conversation from the day before replayed through his mind. "I wish you would," echoing over and over in his thoughts.

"Yes, and from what she said, it's a nasty case. So, whatta ya say? Would you mind covering the meeting? It would really help me out."

"No, of course not. I mean, yes, I'll take care of the meeting. No, I don't mind," Blake replies quickly.

"You're a lifesaver! I'll have everything you need to prepare brought to your office within the hour," Mr. Hayes replies gratefully as he walks down the hall.

Blake robotically gets through the morning and completes Axel's meeting without a hitch. However, he has no idea what he said or how he made it through. He can't stop thinking about the fact that he obviously gave Axel food poisoning.

"Should I feel bad? Cause I sure don't! This day is getting better and better! Axel deserves that and so much more. And I'm going to make sure he gets it."

Blake's newfound confidence continues to grow as he goes about his day, effortlessly completing tasks and handling responsibilities.

During his lunch break, Blake decides to pay a visit to the hospital where Axel is being treated. He walks into the room, his confidence radiating around him like a protective aura. Axel looks pale and weak, hooked up to various machines. He internally groans when he sees Blake.

"Ugh, man, what are you doing here?" Axel croaks out weakly.

"Just thought I'd drop by and see how you're doing," Blake says casually, relishing in the anguish on Axel's face.

"Well, as you can see, not great," Axel mutters. "I don't know what the hell happened last night, but I've never been this sick in my life."

Blake squints slightly and turns his head at Axel's words, a flicker of guilt briefly crossing his features before disappearing behind a smirk. "That's rough, man. Is there anything I can do for you? Need me to pass a message to work or something? I mean, I'm already taking care of your meeting this afternoon."

Axel gives Blake a skeptical look. "You? Helping me out?" He lets out a weak chuckle that quickly turns into a coughing fit. "I think I'll pass on your help, loser. Don't mess up that meeting, either. It's important."

Blake's smug smile widens at Axel's words, ridding him of any lingering guilt. "Oh, don't worry about the meeting. I've got it all covered," he says smoothly, turning to leave the room.

As he walks down the hospital hallway, a sudden thought crosses his mind: What if Axel never recovers from this mysterious illness? What if something were to happen to him while he's in the hospital? The idea sends a thrill down Blake's spine, a rush of power surging through him.

He quickly pushes the thoughts away, reminding himself that he's not capable of such things. But deep down, a dark curiosity begins to stir within him. What other changes could he make in the world around him with this newfound ability? The possibilities seem endless and enticing.

8

CHAPTER EIGHT

Blake's thoughts spiral into a dark and dangerous territory, consumed by the newfound power he holds in his hands. His intentions twist and contort, tainted by a malevolent desire for retribution. As he delves deeper into the sinister possibilities that lay before him, a chill runs down his spine at the realization of what he is becoming. The line between right and wrong blurs as he is seduced by the alluring prospect of using the stone to reshape his world according to his whims.

When he returns to the office, Blake is greeted with a flurry of activity as he prepares for the meeting he is covering for Axel.

As the meeting progresses, Blake effortlessly captures the clients' attention with his ideas and proposals. His confidence is unwavering, and his words are smooth and persuasive. The client hangs on to his every word, nodding in agreement and excitement.

As the meeting concludes, the client expresses enthusiasm for the campaign and praises Blake for his creativity and vision. Mr. Hayes watches from the sidelines, impressed by Blake's performance.

As the clients leave the conference room, talking amongst themselves, Blake heads back to his office, feeling on top of the world. He enters and sets the stone down on his desk, its smooth surface glinting in the dim light of his office. Looking at it now, he sees it as a Pandora's box that he has unwittingly opened. However, the longer he stares at the stone and is drawn to its magnetic pull, the less concerned he is about the consequences of his own thoughts.

The office grows dim as the day progresses, casting shadows that dance around Blake like whispers of temptation. His fingers trace the smooth surface of the stone, its cool touch a stark contrast to the heat that burns within him. The weight of his actions hangs heavy in the air, mingled with the heady scent of power that envelopes him.

A knock at the door startles Blake from his thoughts. Mr. Hayes enters, his face etched with concern. "Blake, are you alright? You seem... different today."

Blake meets Mr. Hayes' gaze with an enigmatic smile. He lifts his shoulders straighter and cocks his head to the left. "Different how, sir?" he inquires innocently, though there is a subtle edge to his tone that doesn't go unnoticed by Mr. Hayes.

"I can't quite put my finger on it," Mr. Hayes admits, studying Blake intently.

"Perhaps I'm finally coming into my own, discovering hidden talents I never knew I possessed," Blake muses cryptically.

Mr. Hayes nods slowly, his piercing gaze fixed upon Blake as he carefully considers his words. Eventually, he shrugs off whatever concern he had and clears his throat before speaking. "I wanted to take a moment to thank you for your excellent work in today's meeting. Your insights and contributions were invaluable." The corner of his mouth curls up into a small smile as he continues, "As you may know, Axel will be out of the office for a few days, and I was wondering if you would be willing to take on some of his responsibilities in the meantime. Your potential and capabilities have not gone unnoticed, and I have full confidence that you have what it takes to handle these additional tasks."

Blake's lips curl into a sly smile, a sense of twisted satisfaction blooming within him. "I would be honored, Mr. Hayes. I'll make sure Axel's work doesn't suffer in his absence."

Mr. Hayes gives Blake a nod of approval before excusing himself from the office, leaving Blake to revel in his newfound sense of power. A malevolent gleam flashes in Blake's gaze as Mr. Hayes exits, and the door clicks shut.

"Keep this moment in mind when you guys are conversing about the promotion," Blake calls after Mr. Hayes. Blake's mind begins to race with dark possibilities. With each passing moment, the allure of power grows stronger, whispering promises of control and dominance. The stone gleams ominously in his hand, a conduit to reshape reality to his will.

His phone vibrates, jolting him back to the present moment. It's a call from his mother. He reaches for the phone and answers it quickly.

"Mom, how's dad? Is everything still okay? Is Aunt Cathy still there with you?"

"Aunt Cathy already left. Your dad is... well, doing just fine," she replies hesitantly.

"What do you mean 'just fine'? What's going on? Why did you stall?" Blake's heart rate starts to pick up as he awaits her response.

"No, nothing is wrong, honey," his mother reassures him. "I'm just still in shock. Right now, your father is walking around the house making a list of projects he wants to get done this week."

Blake can't believe what he's hearing. "What?! Mom and Dad can't be thinking about home renovation projects right now! He just got out of the hospital!"

"I know, dear, but he seems adamant that he can do it. I don't think I can stop him," she admits wearily.

"Mom, please listen to yourself. He collapsed earlier today and had to be taken via ambulance to the hospital!" Blake's worry grows with each passing second.

"Do you think I don't know that? I was the one who saw it happen. Who struggled to get him to the couch. I'm the one who called 911," his mother responds defensively. "The doctors couldn't find anything wrong with him, and honestly, he looks healthier than I've seen him in years. So how do you think I'm going to stop him?"

"Just don't let him overdo it, Mom," Blake pleads with a hint of concern in his voice.

"I'll talk to him, honey, but you know how he is. He might not want to wait for you to help," his mother replies. She knows her husband all too well.

A sudden knock on the door startles Blake, causing him to look up from his desk to see Mr. Hayes once again standing in the doorway.

"Okay, Mom. I gotta go. I'll see you both soon," Blake quickly says on the phone before hanging up. He turns to face his boss, his expression surprised.

"I'm sorry, Blake. I didn't mean to keep barging in like this," Mr. Hayes apologizes as he steps further into the room. "But I have one more favor to ask of you."

"Sure, what is it?"

"Listen, Axel's gone, and Taylor needs help with the

Maxwell campaign. She's drowning in the workload, and the deadline is next week."

Blake's heart races as he remembers that fateful night in the woods. The stone may have erased everyone else's memory of it, but not his. Can he really trust himself to work closely with Taylor?

"If you don't want to, I can ask Matt to step in instead."

Blake's blood boils at the thought of Matt swooping in and taking credit, especially with the promotion on the line. There's no way he'll let that happen.

"No, no, of course I'll help." Blake interrupts quickly, determination showing in his stance.

"That's what I wanted to hear! Taylor will swing by your office tomorrow morning so you two can get started."

Blake nods, the leather of his chair creaking beneath him as Mr. Hayes strides down the hall and disappears from view. The mere thought of working with Taylor would have sent a wave of nausea through him a week ago, but now, with this newfound power flowing through him, all he feels is a bubbling sense of excitement. What kind of revenge can he offer the lovely Taylor? His mind whirs with possibilities, each one more satisfying than the last. He can almost taste the sweet satisfaction that would come with exacting retribution on someone who had wronged him the way she did. A wicked look spreads across his face as he eagerly awaits the opportunity to carry out his plan. With the stone in his possession, he thinks he's invincible.

Blake holds the stone in the palm of his hand, inches away from his face. His lip curling into a wicked grin. "I wish Taylor was obsessed with me."

The stone pulses faintly as Blake's wish swirls into the universe, carried by an unseen force. A sense of anticipation fills the room as he waits for the wish to take effect and his plan to be implemented.

9
CHAPTER NINE

The following day, Taylor arrives at Blake's office promptly at 9 am, a stack of papers in hand. She greets him with a shy grin that catches Blake off guard. He notes the tension in her posture and the slight tremble in her fingers as she hands him the documents. This is a drastic change from her usual confident demeanor around him. Her usually strong and commanding presence has been replaced by one of shyness and nervousness.

"Thank you for agreeing to help me with this, Blake," Taylor says, her voice laced with a hint of apprehension. She tucks a strand of hair behind her ear, an unconscious gesture that reveals her unease. "I know it's short notice, but I really appreciate your help."

In return, Blake offers a congenial smile, though his thoughts are far from innocent. "Of course, Taylor. Happy to lend a hand wherever I can." His features hold a glint of mischief as he takes the papers from her trembling hands.

As they delve into the details of the Maxwell campaign,

Blake notices a subtle shift in Taylor's behavior. She hangs on his every word, admiring his strategic insights and creative suggestions. Blake revels in her newfound admiration and can't help but stoke the flames of her obsession with him.

He deliberately leans in closer to her, his voice seductive as he shares his ideas. Taylor's cheeks flush with embarrassment and excitement, and her gaze locks on his with a newfound intensity. Blake can practically see the invisible threads weaving tighter around her as his wish takes hold.

As the hours tick by, Blake's mind races and churns with ideas until he finally presents one to Taylor. It's a surefire win for the client. He's always known he was good at what he does, but ever since acquiring the stone, his skills have been sharpened to a razor's edge, unleashing an unstoppable force within him. His confidence soars as he finishes detailing his idea for the campaign.

"So, what do you think?" Blake inquires, leaning back in his chair and flexing his toned chest for emphasis.

Taylor's cheeks flush at the sight, and she quickly averts her gaze. She takes a deep breath to compose herself before nodding her head. "I must say, it's a brilliant idea. It aligns perfectly with what the Maxwell Group aims for in this campaign." She can't help but steal a quick glance at Blake, admiring his confident posture and strong presence.

Blake watches as Taylor's gaze lingers on him. A hunger flashes in her eyes, confirming that his wish has taken effect. He recognizes the power he now holds over her, a sensation that sends him a thrill of excitement.

He decides to take things up a notch, knowing he has Taylor right where he wants her. "You know, Taylor, I think we make a pretty good team," Blake says smoothly, leaning in even closer. The air between them crackles with an electric tension that neither can deny.

Taylor swallows nervously, conflicting emotions consuming her. She can't help the magnetic pull drawing her towards him. "I... I think you're right, Blake," she stammers, her voice barely above a whisper.

At that moment, a silent agreement is formed. Both are fully aware of the dangerous game they are playing but for different reasons. The office becomes too small for the intensity of their shared gaze as if the world around them has blurred into insignificance.

Without breaking eye contact, Blake reaches out a hand to gently brush a stray lock of hair away from Taylor's face. Her breath catches at his touch. His fingers linger on her cheek momentarily before pulling back, a sultry smile forming on his lips.

"Taylor," Blake's deep voice breaks through the quiet of their office.

"Yes, Blake?"

He leans in, taking a moment to pause, enjoying his obvious effect on her. "Do you wanna go grab some lunch? I didn't bring anything today, and all this work is making me incredibly hungry."

Taylor's stomach grumbles in response, and she glances down at it, embarrassed. "Oh, ummmmmm."

"Or, if you want, we could order something in so we can keep working on this," Blake suggests, his gaze moving from her face to the piles of papers scattered across his desk.

"Well. I. Uh," she stammers, trying to think quickly. She has never felt this nervous around Blake before, and she can't seem to form words at this moment.

"Together," Blake whispers, leaning back in his chair and meeting her gaze again.

His words send a slight shiver down Taylor's spine, and she

can't help but become flustered by his close proximity. "Whatever you want to do is fine with me."

"Great, then let's just order in and keep at it," Blake decides decisively, standing up and stretching his arms above his head with a satisfied smile. The smell of coffee and worn books fills the air as he walks out of the office to place their lunch order, leaving Taylor both relieved and slightly disappointed that they won't be going together for lunch.

Taylor takes a deep breath, trying to shake off the strange mix of emotions swirling inside her. A man she once despised, she now finds herself drawn to in a way she can't quite comprehend. As she watches him walk out of the office, his confident stride and strong presence leave a lingering impression.

Lost in her thoughts, Taylor absentmindedly flips through the papers on his desk, her mind drifting back to the morning's events. The way Blake looks at her and touches her cheek so tenderly—it all feels too surreal, like a scene from a dream she couldn't quite wake up from.

As Blake returns with their lunch order, Taylor can't help but steal glances at him as they eat. She notices the way his face crinkles when he smiles, the easy confidence in his movements, and the magnetic aura that seems to surround him. Despite her initial reservations about Blake, she can't deny her growing attraction towards him.

Throughout their lunch, they discuss work and personal interests, finding common ground on various topics. Taylor is surprised by how effortlessly they connect, their conversations flowing with a natural rhythm that intrigues and excites her.

As they finish eating, Blake has an idea.

"You know what we need? A break; let's take a short walk outside to clear our minds before diving back into all this," he offers, motioning to the mound of files scattered throughout the room.

"That actually sounds really great. I could use a few minutes to stretch my legs and get some fresh air."Taylor agrees, grateful for the opportunity to step away from the confines of the office.

Outside, the sun shines brightly overhead, casting a warm glow on everything it touches. A gentle breeze rustles the leaves of nearby trees as Blake and Taylor stroll side by side, their steps in sync.

Blake notices the side glances she keeps sneaking and laughs internally, knowing that she would have done anything to be anywhere but in a room with him just a few days ago. Now, she wants him, and there is no denying it. Blake sees Taylor becoming increasingly flustered by his suggestive comments and lingering touches. He relishes in the power he now holds over her, enjoying the way her cheeks flush and her breath quickens whenever he leans in a little too close or lets his hand brush against hers. It's intoxicating, this control he exerts over her reactions.

As they walk, the tension between them grows thicker with each passing moment. Taylor finds herself becoming increasingly entranced by Blake's presence, his every word and gesture sending a thrill down her spine. She struggles to maintain her composure, her heart racing with a mixture of excitement and apprehension.

Blake stops in his tracks, turning to face Taylor with a knowing look. "Taylor," he begins, his voice low and seductive, "there's something I've been wanting to tell you."

Taylor's breath catches in her throat as she waits for him to continue, her gaze locked on his intently.

"I can't shake this attraction between us," Blake confesses, taking a step closer to her. "There's an undeniable connection that I can't ignore any longer."

Taylor's pulse quickens at his words, and her mind reels with the realization of the depth of their mutual attraction. She finds herself drawn to him like a moth to a flame.

Without warning, he reaches out and gently strokes her cheek.

Taylor's breath hitches at his touch. She opens her mouth to speak, but no words come out. Blake leans in closer, his lips hovering just inches from hers. The tension between them crackles in the air, thick with anticipation.

She tries to step back, but Blake's grip on her is firm. His touch sends a shiver down her spine."Blake, what are you doing?" Taylor manages to whisper, her voice barely audible.

Instead of answering, Blake leans in closer, his lips mere inches from hers. The tension crackles between them, the air thick with anticipation.

Before she can make a move, Blake closes the gap between them and captures her lips in a searing kiss. At first, Taylor stiffens in surprise, but soon, she finds herself melting into the kiss, her hands moving up to tangle in Blake's hair. The world around them fades away as they are consumed by the heat of the moment, their bodies pressed close together.

When they finally break apart, both of them are breathless, their hearts racing in sync. Blake looks deeply at Taylor's face, seeing a mix of desire and something else he can't quite place. Without a word, he takes her hand in his and leads her back towards the office building.

As they step inside, Taylor turns to Blake, her expression a whirlwind of emotions. "I... I don't know what just happened," she admits quietly.

Blake smiles knowingly, his face displaying mischief.

"Sometimes unexpected things can turn out to be the best surprises," he replies cryptically.

"Taylor stares at him momentarily before breaking out into a shy smile and turning her face away.

Blake smirks at Taylor's response, a sense of triumph swelling up within him as they enter his office, taking their respective seats and settling in to get more work done. He can't help but relish in the satisfaction of how his plan is unfolding so perfectly.

Despite the whirlwind of emotions swirling inside her, Taylor finds it hard to concentrate on work. Her mind keeps drifting back to the electrifying kiss and Blake's gaze, which seems to see right through her. She can't deny their intense chemistry, a magnetic pull that seems to grow stronger with each passing moment.

On the other hand, Blake appears unfazed by the kiss, his focus unwavering as he dives back into their work. But Taylor notices the subtle glances he sneaks her way every now and then. It's as if he knows something she doesn't.

Hours pass in a blur, papers are shuffled, and emails are sent, but Taylor can't seem to shake off the electric tension that hangs in the air between her and Blake. As evening descends and, the office starts to empty out.

The gentle sound of knuckles rapping on the door breaks the quiet concentration in Blake's office. Their boss, Mr. Hayes, pokes his head through the doorway with a lopsided grin.

"Knock knock, you two planning on working here all night?" he quips, his gaze shifting between Blake and Taylor.

Taylor glances at her watch before turning to Blake with a look of surprise. "Geez, I hadn't realized it was so late."

"We're getting ready to wrap up here and will be heading out soon," Blake replies with a nonchalant shrug.

"It's great to see you two working so well together. I knew

you had it in you, buddy," Mr. Hayes praises as he taps on the door before making his way toward the exit.

As the sound of his footsteps fades away, Blake lets out a sigh. "He's right, let's call it a night. We can finish this up tomorrow."

"Oh, yeah, sure," Taylor responded half-heartedly, her disappointment apparent in her tone.

Blake notices Taylor's disappointment and sees his chance. "Let's go out for dinner before we go back home," he suggests, flashing her a charming smile. It could be our way of celebrating a productive day at work."

She takes a step back in surprise at the unexpected invitation, but a small smile tugs at her lips. "I... I'd like that," she says softly, the hint of a blush coloring her cheeks.

Blake's smile widens at Taylor's acceptance, and he rises from his seat, extending a hand to help her up. As they leave the office behind and step out into the cool evening air, Taylor ponders the sense of anticipation bubbling inside her. She can't quite decipher the enigma that is Blake—his charm, his confidence, his ability to intrigue and unsettle her in equal measure.

They walk side by side to a nearby restaurant, the soft glow of streetlights casting a warm ambiance around them. The clink of cutlery and murmur of diners fill the air as they settle into a quiet corner table. The flickering candlelight dances across Blake's features, highlighting the sharp angles of his jawline and the intensity of his stare.

Conversation flows effortlessly between them, interspersed with shared laughter and moments of comfortable silence. Taylor finds herself opening up to Blake in ways she hadn't expected, sharing stories and dreams as if they had been in a relationship for years.

As the waiter sets down their dessert, Taylor is taken aback when she sees that Blake has remembered what she had said earlier and has ordered her favorite - a rich and indulgent chocolate lava cake. She looks at him with surprise, touched by his considerate gesture. As they both take a bite, savoring the sweet combination of chocolate and the special moment they are sharing, Taylor notices a warmth spreading inside of her that has nothing to do with the romantic atmosphere around them.

She meets Blake's gaze, gratitude evident. "Thank you for this," she finally says.

The moonlight casts a silver glow over the river, and the moving water fills their ears. The gentle rustle of leaves in the breeze accompanies them. The air is cool and crisp, carrying the scent of pine and earth. Blake's hand skims against Taylor's as they walk, sending a tingle down her spine. He reaches for it, and she intertwines her fingers with his. They continue to walk quietly, hand in hand.

They find a bench by the water's edge and sit down, their shoulders almost touching. Taylor watches as Blake gazes out at the river, his profile sharp and defined in the moonlight. As they sit silently overlooking the river, Taylor looks down to see Blake rubbing circles on the back of her hand with his thumb. His touch is gentle yet electric.

Taylor's breath catches at the intimate gesture, her heart thudding in her chest. She meets Blake's gaze, searching for any sign of what he's thinking at this moment. But his expression is unreadable, a mask of calm confidence that both intrigues and unnerves her.

Just as Taylor opens her mouth to break the silence, Blake turns his head to look at her.

Without saying a word, Blake leans in closer, his breath warm against her skin. Taylor's heart flutters in anticipation as he closes the remaining distance between them, his lips brushing against hers in a feather-light kiss.

When they finally break apart, Taylor looks down at her hands. "Blake," she begins, her voice barely above a whisper. "I don't want this night to end."

"Then it shouldn't." Blake's voice is barely a murmur as he leans in once more, capturing Taylor's lips in a kiss that ignites a fire within her.

Time stands still for Taylor as she melts into the kiss, the world around them fading away until there is nothing but the taste of Blake on her lips, the warmth of his touch searing through her. She surrenders to the moment, letting herself be carried away by the intensity of their connection, the unspoken desire that crackles between them like electricity.

A rush of emotions floods through Taylor - desire, confusion, fear.

Blake takes her hand without a word and leads her back towards the city streets, the world around them transformed by the magic of the night.

They continue their walk in silence, their footsteps perfectly synchronized. As they approach the front of their office building, Taylor subtly pulls on Blake's hand, gesturing for them to keep going. Blake cocks an eyebrow and looks down at her suspiciously.

Taylor points nervously at a building just down the street and quietly says, "I live in those condos right over there. Do you want to walk me home?"

Without a word, he nods and intertwines his fingers with hers, leading her towards the direction she pointed. As they walk towards Taylor's condo, the tension between them still crackles in the air but is now mixed with a newfound sense of intimacy.

At this late hour, the streets are quiet, the only sound being the gentle echo of their footsteps against the pavement. Taylor steals glances at Blake as they walk, noticing how the moonlight plays off his features, casting shadows that make him look almost otherworldly.

When they reach Taylor's door, she stops and turns to face Blake. With a deep breath, Taylor hesitantly asks, "Do you wanna come in?"

Blake's gaze meets hers with an unreadable intensity before a slow smile curves his lips. "I thought you'd never ask," he replies, his voice husky with desire.

As they step into Taylor's cozy condo, a boost of nervous excitement fills the room. The air is charged with anticipation as Blake looks around the small space with a curious gleam. Taylor gestures for him to sit on the plush sofa, her heart pounding in her chest.

Blake closes the gap between them without a word, his hands cupping Taylor's face as he leans in to capture her lips in a hungry kiss. Taylor responds eagerly, her hands moving to wrap around his neck as they lose themselves in each other.

The kiss deepens as their passion ignites, and the world around them fades into the background. Taylor's hands tangle into Blake's hair, pulling him closer as if she could never get enough. Every touch and caress sends shivers down her spine, leaving her breathless and wanting more.

Blake's hands trail down Taylor's back, exploring the contours of her body. Taylor's skin tingles at his touch, warmth spreading through her as she surrenders to the moment. The kiss becomes more urgent and heated with each passing second.

The world fades away as they move towards the bedroom, shedding their clothes along the way. Blake's touch ignites a fire within Taylor that she never knew existed, and she surrenders herself completely to the passion that consumes them both.

Blake, who's never been intimate with anyone before, finds his body on fire, every nerve and muscle pulsating with pent-up desire.

He can feel himself nearing the point of release due to the foreplay, and his breaths are coming out in ragged gasps. In a desperate attempt to regain control, he jumps up off the bed and fumbles for his pants, reaching into his pockets and searching frantically for the stone. Taylor comes up behind him, unaware of the internal battle raging within Blake.

"Are you okay?" she asks, placing a comforting hand on his shoulder.

Blake struggles to maintain composure as he finally finds the stone in his pocket. With trembling fingers, he grips it tightly and closes his eyes, silently willing for his wish to come true. "I wish to be a great lover," he thinks with all his might.

But as she takes hold of his hand and presses her body against his, Blake realizes with shock that something has changed. His pleasure no longer overwhelms him; instead, a sense of power and control is coursing through him. "It can't be," he thinks in disbelief. "Did it actually work?"

Blake takes control of their movements with newfound confidence and skill, satisfying Taylor beyond her wildest dreams. And as they collapse onto the bed in a sweaty heap, Blake knows that tonight will be a night neither of them will ever forget.

Hours pass in a blissful haze, their bodies moving together in perfect harmony. As they lay tangled in each other's limbs, their breathing slowing in sync, Taylor turns to Blake, full of warmth and a newfound vulnerability. "I never thought I'd feel like this with anyone," she admits, her voice shaky with emotion.

"I'm sure you didn't," Blake whispers as he untangles himself from her grasp.

Shock and embarrassment cross her face as she attempts to make sense of the situation unfolding.

"Blake, where are you going? What are you doing?"

"I'm getting dressed; what does it look like I'm doing?" He snaps as he pulls his pants up and buttons them quickly.

"Why? You can stay."

"Stay?" He laughs back.

"But... I thought..." Taylor's voice trails off, unable to find the right words to express the whirlwind of emotions running through her. She stands there, wrapped in a sheet, exposed and vulnerable in more ways than one.

"Oh, Taylor. This was purely physical for me," Blake says coldly, his tone cutting through the air like a knife.

The words hit Taylor like a punch to the gut, leaving her breathless. Her heart shatters at his words, the vulnerability she had shown now turning into humiliation. She watches in disbelief as Blake finishes getting dressed, his back turned to her as he prepares to leave without a second glance.

Just as his hand is about to grasp the doorknob, Taylor finds her voice. It's filled with a mixture of hurt and anger. "How could you do this to me?" she demands, her tone wavering slightly.

Blake freezes in his tracks, his hand hovering in mid-air. He turns slowly to face Taylor, raw anger evident as he stares down at her. "I never promised you anything, and I never will," he spits out. "You've treated me like shit for years, acting as if I was worthless and small. All this time, I've endured your cruelty, and now, all of a sudden, you want me. Well, guess what, Taylor? This was all just a twisted game of revenge for me." His voice is laced with venom as he turns away, leaving Taylor to face the harsh truth of his words alone.

Taylor stands there, stunned and speechless, as Blake's words echo in her ears. The truth of his betrayal cuts through her like a knife.

Tears well up in Taylor's eyes, blurring her vision as she processes the depth of his betrayal. Her heart aches with a mix of emotions - anger, disappointment, and hurt all swirling together in a tumultuous storm. "Revenge?" she chokes out, her voice trembling with raw emotion.

Blake shrugs nonchalantly. "Don't make this more awkward than it has to be," he says coolly. "And just so it's not weird at the office tomorrow. You should probably call in sick, and I'll finish up the project for us. I'll make sure it's turned in to Mr. Hayes before the end of the day." His words cut through her like a knife, further cementing his deceit.

Taylor's mind races as she tries to process what's happening. How could he do this to her? The thought of facing him at work tomorrow made her stomach churn.

She watches helplessly as he walks out the door, leaving her alone in the darkness of her empty apartment. The weight of his words settles over her like a suffocating blanket, the truth of his intentions cutting deeper than any physical wound ever could. Taylor sinks to the floor, her sobs echoing in the empty room as she grapples with the betrayal and humiliation she now carries. "This isn't over," Taylor says, anger rising up inside her. She gets up and heads down the hall to the elevator.

Outside, Blake's lips curl into a twisted smirk as he crosses the street and triumphantly strides back to the office. With each step, a surge of exhilaration propels him forward.

"Blake! Get the fuck back over here. You think you can do this to me? No, I do this to you!"

Taylor yells while standing outside her building. Blake turns around, looking at her, and decides to try out this newfound ability to make a wish once again. Taylor continues yelling and walking towards oncoming traffic and stops abruptly. A car horn blasts, but they cannot stop in time, ultimately hitting Taylor.

"I really like this new me," he boasts under his breath, a newfound confidence radiating from his very being as he retrieves his bike. As he hops on and zooms away, he relishes in the knowing of him being unstoppable, fully embracing the new, ruthless version of himself with every pedal.

IO

CHAPTER TEN

Blake struts in with a cocky swagger, his every move exuding confidence and power. He barely spares a thought for Taylor as he sits at his desk, a self-satisfied smirk playing on his lips. The adrenaline from last night's cruel betrayal still thrums, fueling his sense of invincibility as he powers through the day's tasks.

A few hours later, Blake confidently turns in the completed project he and Taylor were working on, offering him a charming smile as he slid the file onto his boss's desk.

"Terrible news what happened to Taylor," says Mr. Hayes. "The good news is she'll be back to work by Friday. Luckily, the car stopped, and the hit wasn't as bad as they thought.

"Yes, thank God," Blake says.

As Mr. Hayes flips through the file, a smile spreads across his face. "I knew having you work with Taylor was a good idea. This is fantastic work.

Blake revels in the praise he receives from Mr. Hayes for a job well done, his ego inflated by his successful manipulation of both the work project and Taylor.

"I hope the additional tasks you've been working on haven't consumed too much of your time and affected your progress on your presentation. There's only one more day," Mr. Hayes muses while closing the file and placing it on his desk.

"Not at all, don't you worry. I'm more than prepared to show off what I think will be a very profitable campaign and earn that new position!"

Mr. Hayes nods approvingly, and Blake excuses himself from his boss's office.

As the day wears on, Blake spends his time in the office basking in the glow of his success, relishing the admiration and praise that come his way. He effortlessly charms his colleagues, and his newfound confidence draws others to him like moths to a flame.

Before long, Blake is watching the office begin to empty out. He takes a quick glance at his watch and realizes it's almost six pm. "Damn, I better get going. Mom's going to be mad if I don't show up for dinner two nights in a row," he grumbles while gathering his things quickly and heading out.

He slings his bag over his shoulder and jumps onto his bike, zipping up his jacket as the wind picks up. "I bet there aren't many more days left this year that I can ride my bike to work."

On the ride home, Blake speeds and maneuvers through traffic, lost in his thoughts and unaware of his surroundings.

Lost in his own self-praising, he didn't notice a car heading towards the intersection he was entering. The sound of tires screeching and a horn blaring startled him back to reality, but it was too late. The car crashed into Blake's bike, launching him through the air.

Blake hits the pavement hard, the impact knocking the wind out of him as he skids across the asphalt. Pain shoots through his body as he tumbles to a stop, his head spinning from the sudden collision. Dazed and disoriented, he struggles to push himself up, his vision blurred and ears ringing from the crash. A warm trickle of blood runs down his forehead, his hands shaking as he attempts to assess the extent of his injuries.

The car driver flings open his door and jumps out. Fear is etched on every line of his face as he runs towards Blake. His eyes widen in shock, and his mouth opens in a gasp as he takes in the sight of what he has just done. "Oh my... are you okay? I'm so sorry. I didn't even see you," he stammers, his hands hovering uncertainly above Blake's body, unsure what to do. His voice is filled with genuine concern and regret.

Blake groans in response, his body aching and head spinning from the impact. However, despite the shock and discomfort, he narrows his gaze. He fixes a steely glare on the driver responsible for the collision, ready to unleash a vicious barrage of expletives in retaliation.

"What the fuck is wrong with you? Do you *not* pay attention when driving? Did you get your license this morning? You could've killed me, you asshole!!"

The driver winces at Blake's outburst, and guilt and fear are evident in his posture. "I'm sorry. I swear I didn't see you! Are you... are you going to be okay?" he stammers, the tremor in their voice betraying their nervousness.

Blake grits his teeth against the searing pain radiating through his body, fueling his rage until it consumes his every thought. He rises to his feet, towering over the trembling driver with an imposing glare filled with raw contempt.

"You have no idea who you just hit," Blake growls, his voice dripping with venom. "I'll make sure you pay for this. But your payment will go far beyond any monetary price. You've just sealed your fate, and it will be a brutal one. You're going to regret ever crossing paths with me," he threatens, his voice low and dangerous.

The driver's eyes widen in fear as he steps back in an attempt to put distance between the two of them while mumbling another apology.

In the distance, Blake hears the wailing sirens of an ambulance as he watches the driver of the car scurrying back to his vehicle, anxiously awaiting the arrival of the police. Blake sees the stone lying on the ground beside his bent-up bicycle as he surveys his surroundings. "It must have slipped out of my pocket," he muses to himself as he limps toward it, his injured leg causing him to wince with each step. Finally reaching down to retrieve the stone, Blake pulls it close to his chest and whispers, "I wish for my body to be completely healed and free from pain." And in that moment, a surge of energy flows through him, starting at his toes and gradually working its way up his body until every ache and pain has vanished, leaving him whole and healed once again. Blake can't help but think about Taylor and the awful pain he's inflicted on her, both emotionally and physically. "Karma really is a mother fucker", he laughs, pain-free.

The police arrive and question the driver while the paramedics check out Blake.

The paramedic's confusion is evident as he examines Blake, who sits nonchalantly on the side of the sidewalk. His bike lay nearby, twisted and mangled from the impact of the accident. But somehow, miraculously, Blake's body shows no signs of trauma. Not a single scratch or bruise could be seen anywhere on his skin.

"How in the world is your bike in such a state, but you are unscathed?" the paramedic asks, dumbfounded.

"Just lucky, I guess," Blake replies with a nonchalant shrug.

The paramedic shakes his head in disbelief.

"If I were you, I'd play the lottery with that kind of luck!" he chuckles.

The police finish questioning the driver and turn to Blake, who is now standing up confidently with a smug grin.

"I'll be fine, officer. No harm done," Blake says, waving away any concerns about his well-being.

As they wrap up the scene and clear the road, Blake retrieves his now-battered bike and inspects it with annoyance.

Once the authorities have gathered all the necessary information, they release the driver with a warning about being more cautious on the road.

As the flashing lights of the emergency vehicles fade into the distance, Blake finds himself standing alone on the sidewalk, the cool evening breeze ruffling his hair. He looks over to see the driver getting in his car, and a sinister smile plays on his lips. His mind races with possibilities, plotting his next move with cold precision. With a calculated gaze, he watches as the driver pulls away from the scene.

"I wish the engine in that car would explode."

In an instant, the unthinkable happens. The driver's car shudders, smoke billows from under the hood, and then, a deafening explosion echoes throughout the air. Blake watches with a twisted sense of satisfaction as chaos unfolds before him, his heart pounding with exhilaration.

The driver stumbles out of his car, coughing and cursing. Gripping the stone tightly in his hand, Blake walks away from the flaming wreckage with a sense of satisfaction. He can hear the cries for help, but his laughter quickly drowns them out.

Returning home to a cold dinner his mother had cooked for him, he sat alone at the table, lost in thought about what had transpired that evening. As he took each bite, he couldn't help but smile.

As Blake finished his meal, he leaned back in his chair, savoring the quiet of the evening. The house was filled with a comfortable silence. His parents were already in bed. But Blake's mind was far from restful. As he sits alone at the table, the events of the last several days replay in his mind like a thrilling movie. He's so engrossed in his own thoughts that he doesn't notice his mother has woken up and is now standing beside him.

She places a hand on his shoulder, which startles Blake and causes him to look up at her in surprise. Her gaze is soft and understanding, filled with the kind of unconditional love only a mother can give.

"Blake, you've been acting strange lately. Is everything alright?" she asks, her voice gentle but firm.

Blake hesitates for a moment, his mind racing with possible explanations. Finally, he decides to go with a half-truth, not wanting to worry his mother further.

"Just some work stress, Mom. It's been a hectic week," he replies, forcing a smile onto his face.

But his mother doesn't look convinced. She studies his face intently as if trying to read his thoughts.

"Are you sure that's all it is? You know you can talk to me about anything, right?" she says softly, her hand squeezing his shoulder reassuringly.

Taking a deep breath, he meets his mother's gaze with a look of feigned weariness. "I promise, Mom, it's just been a tough week at work. What are you doing up anyway?"

"I woke up to pee and wanted to check and see if you had made it home yet. You've been late the last few nights."

"I'm sorry if I was making you worry, Mom, but everything

is fine. It's better than fine, actually," he assures her, reassuringly patting her hand on his shoulder.

His mother nods, though a flicker of doubt lingers. She leans down and kisses Blake's forehead softly before bidding him goodnight and heading back to her room.

As the house falls back into silence, Blake is left alone once again, his thoughts swirling in his mind.

"Who's next?"

The question lingers in the air, heavy with anticipation and a tinge of darkness. Blake's mind races with possibilities, each more exhilarating than the last. He can't deny the rush he gets with each wish granted by the mysterious stone.

"Who's next, indeed."

II

CHAPTER ELEVEN

The following day, after a restless night filled with twisted dreams and dark thoughts, Blake wakes up to the sound of his alarm blaring. He gets up quickly and begins to get ready, eager to see what today will bring.

As he makes his way upstairs, he smells fresh coffee and bacon.

"Mmmm, Mom it smells amazing in here," he praises, joining his parents in the kitchen.

"Thank you, sweetie. Please sit down and eat before you head to work. You only have a few minutes."

"I'm actually going to drive into the office today, so I have some extra time. Dad, what do you have planned for today?"

Blake's question is met with a casual shrug from his dad."Oh, just some yard work, and maybe I'll tinker around in the garage. The usual stuff," his dad replies, a content smile on his face.

"As long as you don't overdo it."

"Don't you worry about me, kiddo; I'm healthy as a horse!" the patriarch offers while beating his chest with his fist.

As they sit down for breakfast, the atmosphere in the kitchen is warm and filled with mundane chatter about the day ahead.

As he finishes breakfast, he stands up and grabs his coat, ready to head out.

"Have a good day at work, Blake," his mother calls out from the kitchen.

"Thanks, Mom. I'll see you both later," he replies with a smile that doesn't quite reach his eyes.

Stepping outside into the crisp morning air, a surge of excitement building within him. As he approached his car, a mischievous smile played on his lips.

"Let's have a little fun today," he whispers to himself as he climbs into the driver's seat. Starting the engine, Blake pulls out of the driveway, driving down the familiar streets of his neighborhood. Blake can't help but wonder what kind of chaos he could create with just a single thought.

Turning onto a quiet road lined with quaint houses, Blake begins to form an idea. He spots an older woman watering her garden and decides on his next target: Mrs. Rose, the neighborhood nosey Nellie. She is always in everyone's business and causing drama. He slows down as he approaches her house, Blake takes a deep breath and whispers his wish, allowing it to flow through him with thrilling electricity.

Within seconds, the older woman tripped and fell, dropping her watering can and causing a clatter when the metal hit the concrete. She looked up, dazed and confused. A younger woman came bursting out of the home, running towards Mrs. Rose and stopping to help her up off the ground carefully.

"Mom, I told you one more fall, and we were going to have to put you in assisted living. I can't be here with you. I'm supposed to fly home today. Who's going to watch over you?" Exasperation is evident in the daughter's voice.

"She ok?" Blake asks.

"Yeah, just mom being mom. Thanks Blake".

Blake rolls up his window and drives off with a smirk of delight.

He continues down the street, the thrill of his newfound power coursing through his veins. As he rounds a corner, he spots a group of teenagers loitering outside the local convenience store. With a wicked grin, he decides to have a bit more fun.

Blake slows down as he approaches them, and with a mere idea, the ground beneath the teens suddenly becomes slick with spilled soda. Chaos ensues as they slip and slide in every direction, their yells of surprise and laughter mixing together in a cacophony of noise.

Blake speeds away from the scene in a rush of exhilaration, his heart pounding with excitement. By the time he reaches the office, Blake is almost giddy and excited about what he will do next.

As he walks through the office doors, he tries to act casually, as if nothing out of the ordinary is happening in his life. But the surge of adrenaline makes it impossible for him to sit still. He can hardly contain his excitement, eager to see what kind of havoc he will wreak throughout the day.

As the workday progresses, Blake finds opportunities to use the stone's power in subtle and not-so-subtle ways. He manipulates stock prices, causing a minor panic among traders. He alters the weather report, resulting in a slew of canceled outdoor event plans. He even interferes with traffic patterns, causing a massive backup that lasts for hours.

Each time he uses the stone, more power fills him. He's become addicted to it, eagerly seeking out new challenges and opportunities to use this power.

Despite his growing obsession with the stone, Blake

manages to maintain his demeanor at work. He monitors the news and social media closely, watching as his actions cause chaos and disruption both in and outside his community.

As he strolls down the hall, Blake feels a sense of authority and control. He passes by Mr. Hayes' office but abruptly stops as he overhears him discussing the upcoming promotion on the phone. Blake creeps closer to the cracked open door to hear better.

"They're both scheduled to present tomorrow, but I must admit that I saw a portion of Matt's presentation earlier today, which was extremely impressive. I'm not sure if Blake will be able to top it." A dangerous gleam enters his gaze as Blake eavesdrops on Mr. Haye's conversation. He can't allow Matt to present tomorrow; that promotion belongs to him.

Blake storms into his office, slamming the door shut behind him. He collapses into his chair, fists clenched and knuckles white with rage. "I'll be damned if I let that incompetent fool beat me," he seethes through gritted teeth. With a quick, furious motion, he pulls out the small stone from his pocket and holds it tightly in his hand. "I wish Matt would never step foot in this office again," his voice drops into a menacing growl, a dangerous intensity flashing on his features as the words escape his lips.

The stone vibrates in his hand, and he knows that promotion is his.

As Blake steps into the office the following morning, a smug satisfaction washes over him. The promotion he has been working towards is now within his grasp, and by the end of the day, it will be his. All thanks to his cunning manipulation of events. He savors the moment.

His footsteps echo through the quiet hallway as he passes Matt's office, taking note of the empty seat at his desk. "I don't expect to see you here again, buddy," he sneers under his breath.

Out of nowhere, Mr. Hayes appears in the hallway, his urgent tone cutting through the hushed conversations of the other staff starting their day.

"If everyone could please meet me in the conference room, there is something very important I need to tell you."

Blake's heart pounds with excitement and nerves as they all file into the room and take their seats. He knows that after the wish he made yesterday, this meeting will bring good news for him. After all, Matt isn't here, so who else could get the promotion? "He must have called and quit this morning," he muses with a smirk.

But as Mr. Hayes clears his throat and begins to speak, a grave expression falls upon his face—the atmosphere in the room shifts from eager anticipation to somber tension.

"I regret to inform you all that Matt is no longer with us," he says solemnly. "He was involved in a fatal car accident this morning on his way to work." A collective gasp fills the room as this heartbreaking news sinks in.

Blake must force himself to contain his grin as the silence stretches on. Everyone in the room is in shock and disbelief. Several of his co-workers are now crying. However, while he had no intention when he made his wish for Matt to die, it was very convenient. He's finally getting what he deserves. He's not just getting a promotion; he's rid the company of an incompetent fool who had been standing in his way—a sense of satisfaction courses through him.

"Well, that went a little further than I had intended," Blake thinks to himself smugly.

The room is silent as everyone takes in the news. Slowly, they begin to disperse, full of grief.

Mr. Hayes stays behind to talk to Blake, the only one remaining in the conference room.

"Blake, I don't know what to say." Mr. Hayes's voice trembles with sadness and disbelief. Matt was such a valued member of our team, and this is all just so sudden."

Blake nods, trying to appear sympathetic. "I know, Mr. Hayes. It's just so unexpected and tragic," he says quietly. We had only recently begun getting along, and now I'll never have the chance to bond with him."

"I'm sorry, Blake. Please excuse me," Mr. Hayes chokes out as he turns toward the door. He leaves the room to compose himself. Blake watches after him nonchalantly. He doesn't have time for guilt—he's got a promotion to claim.

With renewed determination, he strides out of the conference room and heads toward his desk. As he passes by others in the office, they shoot him sympathetic glances, but Blake dismisses them with a curt nod. His mind is focused solely on the prize that awaits him at the end of this day.

Once he arrives at his desk, he sends a quick email to Mr. Hayes confirming his availability for the presentation – Matt's absence has sealed the deal, and Blake knows that he will be crowned as the new shining star of the company.

Blake's heart is pounding, and he can barely contain his excitement. He begins tweaking slides and revising his outline; he wants it to be flawless. In the middle of this work, he hears the familiar ding of a new email. It's from Mr. Hayes, so he clicks on it instantly.

Thank you for offering to continue with the presentation today. However, given everything that's happened, we have decided to cancel that meeting and let anyone who wants to go home and grieve today do so.

With that said, I want to let you know that the board and I just had a conversation, and we are going to offer you the new position. It will start immediately. Under the circumstances of the day, if you wish to take the rest of the day off, you can.

Blake's heart pounds with excitement as he re-reads the email, commitment and false sincerity evident in his response to his boss:

I appreciate the offer to leave for the day during this difficult time. Matt's passing truly grieves me. However, I think staying here and continuing to work would benefit me the most. This would allow me to keep my mind occupied and not focused on the tragedy.

I am also honored to have this new opportunity. I will do everything I can to ensure our company continues to excel. Thank you for your trust and confidence; I will not disappoint you.

With that, Blake closes the email and exhales a sigh of relief. He can now bask in the joy of knowing he got precisely what he wanted.

He spends the afternoon rearranging his office, setting up new files, and organizing his workspace.

As the day wears on, a timid knock echoes through the door of Blake's office. Slowly lifting focus from the papers scattered across his desk, he catches sight of the most mesmerizing woman he's ever seen. He is rendered speechless by her beauty.

"I apologize for disturbing you, especially during such a difficult time. I was supposed to attend your presentation today. I flew in and came straight here, unaware of what happened to your colleague. My sincerest condolences."

Blake can only nod in shock, unable to form words as he takes in the ethereal being before him. Her presence fills the room with a sense of grace and elegance that leaves him breathless.

Her every word entrances Blake as she continues to speak.

The warmth and sincerity in her voice seem to emanate from her very soul, and a strange, unfamiliar warmth swirls in his chest in response.

He finally finds his voice and manages a response. "Thank you... my name is Blake. It's...it's really nice to meet you."

The woman smiles warmly back at him, a genuine delight apparent as she replies, "I'm Katarina. It's such an honor to finally meet you, Blake. I've heard so much about you and your work. I was really looking forward to seeing the presentations today."

As Katarina speaks, her eyes lock with his in a magnetic gaze. His heart starts to race, the sound of it pounding in his ears. Although she is here as a representative for her company, Blakes recognizes an immediate connection to her.

Katarina's presence radiates an electrifying energy that fills the air around him. Every word she speaks and every movement she makes captivate him. He can't help but notice the fine hairs on his arms stand up straight as if responding to her powerful aura. Her alluring gaze so entrances him that he barely registers what she says about the presentation and her upcoming travel plans.

Katarina's voice breaks through Blake's dazed state, snapping him out of his stupor. He blinks a few times, trying to focus on her words as she asks him a question. But his mind is blank, and he can't recall anything she just said. "I'm sorry," he says apologetically, "can you repeat the last part? I faded out. It's been a long day."

Katarina's face twists with guilt as she realizes her mistake. "Oh my goodness, how foolish of me. Of course, it can wait. We can go over your presentation another time." Her voice is filled with genuine remorse.

But before she can turn away, Blake's sudden shout startles her, and she takes a step back in surprise.

"NO!" he exclaims, his tone sharp and desperate. I mean... no, it's alright. You're already here, so let's go over things now."

Katarina hesitates for a moment before nodding. "Alright, let's do it."

Katarina pulls up a chair next to Blake's desk, her presence still casting a spell over him. As they begin reviewing the presentation, Blake finds himself effortlessly drawn into the conversation. Katarina's insights and suggestions are like beams of light illuminating his ideas, helping them shine brighter than ever before.

A drop of blood drips onto a piece of paper in front of Katarina. She instantly covers her nose. Instinctively, Blake grabs a tissue from his desk and hands it to her.

"Are you okay? Your nose is bleeding!"

"Yes, I'm sorry. This is so embarrassing. It's been doing that all day. Honestly, it's been doing it a lot over the last few weeks. I've been to the doctor. They can't find a reason for the bleeding. It just starts happening randomly."

"Are you sure you're okay?" Blake asks, his voice laced with genuine worry.

Katarina nods, a faint smile gracing her lips despite the trickle of blood staining the tissue. "It's nothing to worry about, just a nuisance more than anything."

"Well, I suppose as long as the doctors can't find anything wrong, it must be okay. Maybe it's from dry air or something."

"I'm sure. Would you excuse me for a minute? I'm going to run to the bathroom to clean this up. It really is embarrassing. I can't apologize enough."

"No apology necessary!" Blake reassures.

As he watches her walk down the hall, he has an idea. In thought, "I wish Katarina's nose would stop bleeding and heal whatever is causing them."

With a massive grin, he waits for her to return to his office.

The minutes tick by slowly as Blake anxiously awaits Katarina's return.

Finally, Katarina walks through the door, but Blake's excitement quickly turns to confusion when he sees a tissue shoved in her right nostril.

"Sorry," she apologizes sheepishly, noticing his confused expression. "It got worse while I was out there."

Blake's in disbelief as he processes what she just said. "What?" he exclaims, causing Katarina to jump back in surprise. Quickly realizing how loud he was, he reaches out and gently touches her shoulder. "I didn't mean to startle you," he says softly. "I'm just surprised. I assumed for sure it would have cleared up.

"Yeah, me too."

Blake's mind races as he struggles to comprehend the unexpected turn of events. His attempt to use the stone's power to help Katarina didn't work. The only time he had experienced a wish not working was when he made the wish for his appearance, and the stone wasn't on him. It was on the counter, and then when he made the wish the second time in front of the mirror, he had the stone in his pocket, and it worked. Only he had the stone on him this time, and it still didn't work.

Perhaps he's worn out his wishes? Maybe he's doing something wrong. A nosebleed can't be beyond the stone's power, could it? He healed his father. Why can't he do the same for her? Unsure of what's going on, he decides against making the same wish for a third time.

As if on cue, Katarina releases a small gasp and puts her hand on her nose. Blake's heart skips a beat as he watches the scene unfold in real-time. The tissue in her nose is now completely soaked in blood.

As panic threatens to overtake him, Blake's mind races for a solution. Despite his initial confidence in the stone's power, the unexpected lack of healing from his wish has left him reeling.

"Listen, I am again so sorry about this. I'm going to go ahead and go to my hotel. I didn't mean to take up your day anyway. I just wanted to introduce myself and offer my condolences for the loss of your colleague."

"No, I was happy to discuss the campaign with you and would love to continue this conversation. Would it be possible to meet later tonight?"

A sly smirk plays on her lips as she suggests a location, "How about the rooftop restaurant at the Montego Resort and Spa? That's where I'm staying tonight."

He takes note of her confident demeanor as she hands him her number, "I'll call you when I leave here," he promises.

"The stone didn't work on her," he muses as he watches her walk down the hall toward the exit. "Interesting."

12

CHAPTER TWELVE

Later that evening, a soft breeze rustles the leaves as Blake makes his way up to the rooftop restaurant at the Montego Resort and Spa. The sound of laughter and clinking glasses fills the air, creating a vibrant atmosphere under the starlit sky. He spots Katarina sitting at a corner table, her silhouette illuminated by the gentle glow of string lights overhead.

As he approaches, she looks up and smiles warmly, gesturing for him to take a seat—the candlelight flickers, giving them a gleam that captivates him once more.

"Thank you for coming," she says, her voice velvety smooth. "I hope you don't mind me choosing this place for our meeting."

Blake shakes his head, his gaze fixed on her. "Not at all. It's beautiful."

They engage in effortless conversations about topics ranging from work to personal interests. Katarina's words are like music to his ears, and each sentence draws him closer to her.

Blake finds himself enchanted by Katarina's presence and charisma.

As the night wears on, they find themselves lost in the moment, the world around them fading into the background. The rooftop restaurant becomes their own private sanctuary, filled with shared laughter and meaningful glances.

In a daring move, Blake reaches out to gently take Katarina's hand, his heart pounding with a mixture of nerves and excitement. To his relief, she intertwines her fingers with his.

Their hands fit together perfectly as if they were always meant to find each other at that exact moment. And as they sit there, bathed in the warm glow of the night and each other's company.

Blake meets her gaze with a heavy sigh—his features show longing and sadness. "I wish you weren't leaving in the morning," he says, sounding more like a plea than a statement.

Katarina's expression softens as she hears his words, a flicker of emotion crossing her features. She squeezes his hand gently, her eyes searching his for a moment before she speaks.

"I wish I didn't have to leave either," she says softly, her voice carrying a hint of regret. "But duty calls, and I have to return home tomorrow."

There's a moment of silence between them, filled with unspoken words and swirling emotions. Blake wrestles with the weight of their impending goodbye, which hangs in the air, casting a shadow over the otherwise perfect evening.

"I wish things were different," he murmurs, his thumb tracing small circles on the back of her hand. "I wish we had more time."

Katarina nods, a wistful smile tugging at her lips. "Me too," she replies, her voice barely above a whisper. "But perhaps...perhaps this isn't goodbye forever."

Blake's heart fills with hope at her words, but it quickly

dissipates as her cell phone buzzes. She pulls it out of her purse and checks the notification.

"It's my boss, do you mind?"

"No, not at all. Go ahead," he tells her, leaning back in his chair.

"Christopher...yes, I did actually..." her voice trails off as she turns and walks away from the table.

After several long minutes, she returns to their table with a perplexed look etched on her face. Blake's instant concern is evident in his furrowed brow and tense posture.

"Is everything okay?" he asks, leaning forward.

She shakes her head, still lost in contemplation. "You're not going to believe this," she begins, her voice tinged with disbelief.

"What is it?"

"They're opening a branch office out here, and they want me to run it," she says, absentmindedly playing with the hem of her shirt. "My boss asked me to stay a few more days to finalize a few things here. I'll need to relocate next month."

Blake's jaw drops as he listens to her words. He realizes that in his moment of sadness earlier, he had made a wish for her to stay without even realizing it. It never occurred to him at that moment to wish her to stay, and yet he did.

"So the stone does work on her," he muses.

But before he can respond, his gaze is drawn upwards, and he notices that her nose has started bleeding again.

Katarina reaches up to touch her nose, a look of frustration crossing her features as she sees the blood on her fingertips.

Blake's heart lurches at the sight, his mind racing for a solution. Without a second thought, he grabs a napkin from the table and offers it to Katarina.

"Here, use this," he says urgently. "Hold it against your nose, and tilt your head up."

Katarina nods gratefully, pressing the napkin to her nose with a shaky hand. The crimson stain seeping into the paper, a stark contrast against the pristine white. She takes a few deep breaths.

"I'm so sorry. I don't know why this is always happening. I'm so embarrassed," she sighs as she excuses herself and hurries off to the restroom to tend to the nosebleed, leaving Blake alone at the table.

After waiting a few more minutes, his phone dings to notify him of a new message. It's from Katarina:

I apologize, Blake. I think I'm just going to head up to my room for the night. I'll stop by your office sometime tomorrow. Thank you for a lovely evening.

Blake replies back quickly.

Katarina, I understand. Please take care and get some rest. I look forward to talking with you at the office tomorrow. Sleep well.

The night air was cool as Blake walked down the hall towards his car after settling the bill.

Blake gets home late that night, his mind still whirling with dreams of Katarina and their brief but memorable encounter. A wide grin of pure bliss spreads across his face as he lies on his bed, staring at the ceiling. "I'm going to spend the rest of my life with her," he thinks to himself with certainty.

Over the next several months, Blake and Katarina spend endless hours on the phone, their voices filling the space between them with laughter and longing. They take turns flying back and forth to see each other, and every trip is like a dream come true. What began as a simple business arrangement has now flourished into a passionate love story that neither of them could have predicted. The distance only makes their hearts grow fonder, and they seize every moment they have together, cherishing every touch and kiss as if it were their last.

Their relationship was like a flower, blooming with every passing day. They laughed, cried, and talked about their hopes and dreams for the future. They knew their love was unique—all-consuming, passionate, and utterly unquantifiable.

One day, as they sit on the rooftop of another restaurant, gazing at the stars and dreaming of their future together, Katarina turns to Blake with a sparkle that rivals the twinkling lights in the sky.

"I have an idea," she whispers, taking his hand and intertwining their fingers again. "What if we... what if instead of me moving into the apartment, we move in... together?"

"What if... you marry me?" he replies, his nerves evident in his shaky voice. Blake's heart swells with happiness and anticipation as he waits for her answer. Looking into her eyes, he envisions all the amazing possibilities that lie ahead for them. He sees a future full of joy and affection, filled with exciting journeys and intense love.

As the words leave his lips, she meets his gaze and smiles warmly, shining with a mix of emotions. "Yes," she says softly, nodding her head in agreement.

HE PULLS her close and holds her tightly, pushing the warmth from her body against his. The night air is cool against their skin as they bask in the glow of their love and commitment to each other.

"I can't wait to start our lives together," he says, his voice thick with emotion.

The night passes quietly, filled with whispers of love and shared dreams of a future together. They discuss marriage and buying a house together—one big enough that his parents could live in their basement instead of vice versa. They discuss baby names for future children. Blake falls asleep peacefully, knowing that he has found the love of his life. The last thing he remembers before drifting off is wishing always to feel this way.

It wasn't until he got up to get ready for the day that he noticed the red stain on her pillow.

"Babe?"

"Yes? Katarina calls from the bathroom.

The pale morning light filtered through the bathroom window, casting a soft glow on Katarina as she walked out in a towel.

Looking at Katarina and holding the pillow, Blake asks, "Another one?"

She shrugged nonchalantly at Blake's question, "Yeah."

He furrowed his brow with concern, "You told me that you haven't been getting those anymore?"

"I haven't," she reassured him, "Last night was the first one I've had in weeks. But I forgot my nasal spray for this trip, so I haven't used it in a few days."

Relief floods over Blake's face as he exclaims, "Why didn't you say so? We gotta get you more today!"

Katarina let out a small chuckle. "Because I didn't even think about it until last night when it started bleeding. Then I remembered that I hadn't packed it." With a sigh, she added, "Since I'm flying back home in a few hours, I'll just use it when I get there. There's no sense in going to get more now."

Blake pulled her closer to him and pouted playfully, "I don't want you to go home." The warmth of his embrace and the familiarity of their playful banter eased any lingering worries about her nosebleed.

With a smile plastered on her face, she lovingly kisses his lips and exclaims, "In case you forgot, we are going to be living together soon!" Her excitement could hardly be contained as she dreams about their future together. "I need to go home and tell my parents I'm getting married!"

He hugs her tightly, relishing the love and excitement radiating from her. "That's right, we are!" he whispers into her ear. The idea of spending the rest of his life with Katarina fills him with pure happiness. The future seems brighter than ever, and he can't wait to start their journey together.

Katarina leaves for the airport, and Blake heads upstairs. Excited to tell his parents about his engagement. They've spent time with Katarina a handful of times whenever she is in town, and they have only ever had wonderful things to say about her.

Blake enters the living room to find his father standing at the top of a tall ladder, carefully patching a hole in the ceiling. The familiar scent of sawdust and paint filled the air, along with the faint sound of a radio playing in the background.

"Dad, what in the world are you doing?" Blake asks incredulously.

"Your mother saw a spider," was his father's nonchalant reply.

"That gives me more questions than answers. Again, what are you doing? And where is mom?"

Blake's mom walks around the corner and wraps her arms around her son as if on cue.

"I never get to see you anymore. You're always with Katarina or working these days," she says wistfully.

"I know, Mom, I'm busy. But listen, there's something important I want to talk to you and Dad about."

"Oh, get off the ladder, Bill. This doesn't sound good," his mom says as she sits on the couch.

"Now, why would you think that, Mom? This is actually really good news," Blake reassures her.

"In that case, Bill, get off the ladder! We need to celebrate!" his mom exclaims excitedly.

"I'm coming, I'm coming," their father grumbles as he carefully steps down and sets his tools on the floor. "Alright, what is it, son?"

"Mom, Dad, you're going to get the daughter you've always wanted!" Blake exclaims, clapping his hands together in front of himself with excitement. His mother's brow furrows in confusion. "What? I've never expressed a desire for a daughter," she replies, her voice tinged with bewilderment.

Blake shakes his head in frustration. "Mom, please listen to what I'm saying." He takes a deep breath before continuing. "I asked Katarina to marry me, and she said yes!"

His mother stares back in shock. "You two have only known each other what six months give or take. Probably less!" she exclaims, her concern evident in her tone. "You can't possibly consider marrying someone you've only known for such a short time!"

"Mom, you and Dad got married after three months!" Blake retorts, trying to defend his decision.

"That was different!" his mother protests.

"How is it different?" Blake challenges, hurt by his mother's lack of enthusiasm. "And why aren't you happy for me? I thought you liked Katarina!"

"I do like her, and I am happy for you," his mother reassures him. "I just think this is all happening too fast. I don't want to see you get hurt."

Blake sighs heavily, understanding that his mother's worries are rooted in care and concern. However, he is confident in his strong bond with Katarina and is ready to move forward with their relationship.

Blake glances back and forth between his parents, completely taken aback. He was sure they would share in his excitement, but their reactions are completely opposite of what he anticipated.

"I can't deal with you right now," Blake snaps, his anger boiling over as he storms off toward the basement. His fists clench so tightly that his knuckles turn white, and his jaw is set in a hard line.

"Blake, wait! Please, just talk to me for a minute," his mother pleads, her voice shaking with hurt and confusion.

But Blake doesn't want to hear it. He spins around to face his mother, venom dripping from his words. "I have nothing left to say to you. Just leave me alone."

"You don't mean that, Blake," she says. "Baby, I'm just looking out for you."

Blake turns towards his mother. "How many times am I going to tell you I'm not a baby!" His anger has taken control, and he's gone completely blind.

"It's your fault I'm like this. I'm not normal. I've always been the weird kid. You two always enabled my behavior. I've always felt like I didn't belong, and when I come to you, you say it's perfectly fine. IT WASN'T FINE MOM! I was the one getting beat up and bullied, not you. Now, when I finally find some resemblance of happiness in my life, you... you... Blake starts walking up the stairs, and his mother follows.

"Blake, we need to talk this out," she cries as tears run down her cheeks.

Blake, on top of the stairs, turns around and yells, "I wish you would just go away and leave me alone! At that moment, Blake realizes what he just said and what that means.

The words had flown out of Blake's mouth before he knew what he was saying. A knee-jerk statement made in anger that he knows will have dire consequences. He reaches out to grab his mother, but it's too late. Time stands still as he watches his mother lose her footing and tumble down the stairs, her body contorting at unnatural angles until she lands at the bottom with a sickening thud.

For a moment, Blake is paralyzed with shock, unable to speak or move. But then reality sets in, and he races to his mother's side, tears streaming down his face as he begs for forgiveness. It's too late, though - his words have already caused irreparable damage, and everything has changed in an instant.

Hearing the noise and commotion, his father comes running down the stairs.

"What happened? Martha! Martha, wake up, honey!"

"I wish my mom was healed and healthy. I wish my mom was healed and healthy. I wish my mom would wake up. I wish my mom was awake," Blake yells at the top of his lungs. Wishing for the stone to heal his mother as it had once done not long ago for his father. But there is no pulsating coming from the stone. There is no ambient light. There is only the sound of the wailing coming from his father.

Blake's heart feels like it's being ripped from his chest, each beat sending searing pain through his body. He watches helplessly as his father cradles his mother, tears streaming down their faces. The air is thick with panic and fear, suffocating him as he realizes the effect caused by his harsh words to his mother. He can't bear to look as the paramedics load her lifeless body onto a gurney and cover her with a cold sheet.

He knows that this tragedy is entirely his fault, and he can do nothing but watch in horror and despair as his actions lead to the death of the one person who loved him unconditionally.

13
CHAPTER THIRTEEN

Tears blur Blake's vision as he tries to process the magnitude of what has just occurred. His mind is a whirlwind of regret and self-loathing as he replays the harsh words he spoke to his mother over and over again. How could he have been so cruel? How could he have let his anger consume him to the point where irreversible damage was done?

As the reality sinks in, a heavy silence settles over the house, broken only by the sound of his father's grief-stricken cries. Blake knows that this tragedy will haunt him for the rest of his days, a constant reminder of the consequences of his actions.

Hours pass in a blur of grief and disbelief. Blake sits numbly on the basement stairs, staring blankly at the spot where his mother fell. The darkness seems to swallow him whole, engulfing him in a sea of overwhelming emotions.

Blake's mind is a whirlwind of regret and anguish as he struggles to come to terms with the reality of what he has done. The memory of his mother's last moments plays on a loop in his mind. Each word he spoke to her, a sharp dagger in his heart. He knows that he can never take back his actions and never undo the pain he has caused. As night falls and darkness envelops the house, Blake remains frozen on the stairs, his body racked with sobs of grief and guilt. The weight of his mother's absence hangs heavily in the air.

Days pass, each one blending into the next in a haze of funeral arrangements, condolences, and unrelenting grief. The weight of sorrow hangs over Blake like a heavy fog, obscuring his mind and clouding his vision.

Haunted by the memory of that fateful moment in the basement, his mother's lifeless form is etched into his mind forever. The anger in his voice echoes through his ears, a constant reminder of his own destructive actions. And as he stands at her graveside, surrounded by Katarina, family, and friends, Blake is consumed by an overwhelming sense of loss.

Tears stream down his face as the priest utters a prayer for his mother's soul. The weight of his guilt threatens to crush him, suffocating him in remorse as he stares at the freshly dug grave. Each shovelful of dirt hitting the coffin is like a punch to his heart.

As friends and family offer empty words of condolence, Blake is consumed by a numbness that engulfs him entirely. His father sits in silence, lost in his own grief and unable to provide any comfort. The once lively and warm household is now hollow and desolate.

"Can I make you something to eat?" Katarina asks softly, concern evident. It has been days since the funeral, but Blake can't find the strength to leave his bed. Katarina has been his rock, tirelessly caring for both him and his father day and night. But even her unwavering support can't ease his burden of guilt.

"I'm not good enough for you. It would be best if you left

before I hurt you, too," Blake says, his voice cracking as he looks at Katarina.

"Blake, I'm not going anywhere. Not now, not ever," she whispers, running her fingers gently along his back.

Despite his self-loathing and guilt, her presence brings him peace and hope in his shattered world. She is the one constant in the chaos, the one person who sees past his mistakes and stands by him unconditionally. Her touch is a balm to his wounded soul, a reminder that there is still goodness in the world despite the darkness threatening to consume him.

Blake's voice trembles as he speaks, his words weighed down by heavy emotion. "Katarina, I'm sorry for everything. I never intended for any of this to happen."

She reaches out and gently strokes his cheek, her touch bringing a sense of comfort and warmth. "It wasn't your fault, Blake. What happened was a tragic accident."

He shakes his head, tears streaming down his face. "But it is my fault. I said those terrible things to her. I pushed her away. And now she's gone."

Katarina wraps her arms around him, holding him tight as he sobs uncontrollably. "No, Blake. Listen to me. Your mother loved you more than anything in this world. She knew you loved her too, even in your moments of anger. She wouldn't want you to blame yourself for what happened." Her words are like a soothing balm to his broken heart, offering solace amid his grief. But only he knew that no matter what she said, it was one hundred percent his fault.

As days turn into weeks, Blake finds himself caught in a relentless cycle of guilt and sorrow. The house that had once been filled with warmth and laughter is now cold and empty, haunted by his mother's absence. Every corner holds a memory—every room echos with her laughter, a constant reminder of the irreparable loss he has caused.

Katarina has stayed by his side through it all, a source of unwavering support and love. She holds him when he can't stop the tears from falling, listens when he needs to talk, and stays silent when there are no words left to say. Her presence is a lifeline in his stormy sea of emotions, guiding him through the darkest moments with her quiet strength.

The day began like any other, but as Blake sits on the edge of his bed, he's consumed with a desperate desire for the pain to end. Ever since his mother's passing, he's kept the stone in a box under his bed, trying to avoid its tempting call. But in this moment, he can no longer resist. The stone beckons him to hold it, and he finds himself reaching for the box and slowly opening it.

As he pulls out the stone and holds it in his hands, a warmth spreads throughout his body. And in that moment, Blake becomes instantly invigorated.

"I just wish the pain and guilt would go away," he whispers to the stone. Light begins to radiate from the stone, enveloping him in its warm glow. Within seconds, the heavy weight of guilt and sadness lifts from him. He no longer feels guilty about what happened to his mother; in fact, it's as if the stone has left him indifferent to the situation.

"Babe," he calls out, searching for Katarina. She emerges from the bathroom, her expression filled with concern.

"Are you alright?" she asks slowly.

"I'm great. Let's go grab something to eat."

"Oh, you're hungry. I can make you something. What do you want?"

"No! I don't want you to make me something. I want us to get out of this house and go eat," he snaps back.

Katarina takes a step back in shock, Blake has never raised his voice at her.

He "is instantly filled with regret. I'm sorry, baby; I didn't mean to speak to you like that."

"It's fine; I get it; you're still grieving. Let's do this. You get ready, and I'll quickly check on your dad upstairs. Meet me there when you're done."

He watches her run up the stairs, a pang of guilt in his chest. He knows he hurt her, and that is the last thing he would ever want to do. He ruminates on the fact that he's unworthy of her love as he enters the bathroom.

While standing at the toilet, he notices bloody tissues in the trash can. "At this point, it seems like that is just going to be a lifelong problem," he concludes with a heavy sigh while washing his hands and heading upstairs to join her.

Blake immediately locks in on Katarina, sitting on the couch as he reaches the top of the stairs. She appears tense, her hands clasped tightly in her lap, and her lips pressed into a thin line. His heart constricts with worry as he approaches her.

"Hey, are you still mad at me?" he asks, sitting beside her.

Katarina lets out a sigh and turns to face him. "No, not at all. There's just something I want to talk to you about when we get to the restaurant."

Dread washes over him as he hears her words. He knows he's been distant lately, pushing her away in fear of hurting her like he hurt his mother. Now, it seems like she's finally had enough and is going to leave him.

"Please, Katarina," he begs, his heart shattering into a million pieces. "Don't leave me. I'll do better, I promise."

She quickly reassures him, "No, no, it's nothing like that."

Relief floods through him but is quickly replaced by curiosity and apprehension. "Then what is it? Just tell me now. I can't wait until we get to the restaurant."

Taking a deep breath, Katarina looks directly into his pleading eyes and takes a deep breath.

"Blake, I'm pregnant."

"Pregnant?" he echoes, the word sounding foreign and unreal on his tongue. He searches Katarina's face for any sign of doubt or hesitation, but all he sees is raw vulnerability and a flicker of hope.

Katarina nods slowly. "I just found out this morning. I didn't want to overwhelm you, but I couldn't keep it from you either."

A wave of emotions crashes over Blake as he takes in the magnitude of her words. A surge of protectiveness and love well up within him, mingling with the persistent guilt that has become a constant companion since his mother's passing.

"I... I don't know what to say," he stammers, reaching out to take Katarina's hand in his. "This is... unexpected, but it's also amazing. We're going to have a baby."

A tear slips down Katarina's cheek, and she nods, a mix of emotions playing on her face. "I know it's a lot to take in, especially with everything you've been through lately. I was so afraid to tell you, Blake. I wasn't sure how you would react."

He leans in and gently kisses her forehead. "I may not have all the answers, but one thing I'm sure of is that I love you, and I want this baby. I want us to make a family."

A soft smile graces Katarina's lips as she buries her face in his chest, a mix of relief and joy washing over her.

As they sit together on the couch, hand in hand, a profound sense of peace settles between them. For the first time in what seems like an eternity, Blake allows himself to imagine once again a future filled with love, laughter, and now also the pitter-patter of tiny feet.

Blake's voice radiates excitement and joy as he shouts, "We're going to have a baby!" His happy exclamation echoes throughout the house.

From the other room, Blake's father calls out, "What? What's going on out there? Who's doing what?"

Amidst fits of giggles between both Blake and Katarina, Blake finally replies as his dad enters the room, "You're going to be a grandpa, Dad!"

There is a moment of stunned silence before Blake's father whispers, "A grandpa?!"

Katarina's laughter bubbles over as she confirms, "A grandpa."

The air is filled with overwhelming love and anticipation as they share this exciting news with Blake's father.

Blake's father gasps in disbelief, his weathered face breaking into a wide grin. He crosses the room in a few strides and envelops both Blake and Katarina in a bone-crushing hug. Tears well up as he whispers, "I can't believe it... I'm going to be a grandpa."

A swell of emotion rises in Blake's chest as he watches his father wipe away a stray tear. At that moment, he is filled with a deep sense of gratitude for the opportunity to create new memories and build a future with his growing family. Katarina coughs and excuses herself from the two, going into the kitchen and getting herself a glass of water. However, when she takes a sip, she grimaces. It has a strange taste. She looks at her glass and then touches her lips. Pulling her hand away from her mouth, she gasps at the sight of blood on her fingertips. She's now coughing up blood.

14

CHAPTER FOURTEEN

As each morning dawned, Katarina's hands instinctively went to her swollen belly, feeling the tiny flutters and kicks from within. Her clothes no longer fit comfortably, and she had to constantly readjust as her round belly grew bigger with each passing week. But with every movement from her little one, she couldn't help but smile at the miracle growing inside of her.

Despite their initial plans for a big, fancy wedding ceremony, they ultimately decided to exchange their vows in a small courthouse ceremony. They both agreed that saving up for a house for their new family was more important than an extravagant celebration.

So today, as they stand hand in hand at the courthouse, Katarina can't help but feel overwhelmed with love and excitement for the future ahead. The sun shines down on them, casting a warm glow over the momentous occasion. And as they recite their vows and affirm their commitment with a kiss, they know that this is just the beginning of their journey together.

The judge's voice echoes through the courthouse as he proclaims them husband and wife. Katarina's grip tightens on Blake's hand, her nails digging into his skin. He starts to question her strength until he sees her face contorted in pain.

"What's wrong?" Blake asks, turning towards his new bride.

But before she can answer, a gush of water spills onto the floor beneath her feet.

The judge's jaw drops as he quickly pushes back his chair, looking frantically for any sign of a medical professional. "You better get going, son! She can't have that baby in here," he chuckles, ushering them out of the courthouse.

As he helps Katarina into the car, adrenaline courses through Blake's veins, his mind a blur of purpose and emotions. They speed through the streets, and Katarina's contractions grow stronger and closer with each passing minute. With each contraction that wrecks Katarina's body, Blake whispers words of encouragement and love, his voice steady despite the chaos around them.

Blake's car screeches to a halt in front of the entrance, the smell of burning rubber filling the air. He leaps out and sprints to her door, yanking it open and frantically calling for assistance. A nurse appears and quickly grabs a wheelchair. With practiced ease, she helps the laboring woman into the chair.

"I'll go park the car; I'll be right back, baby," Blake promises, his voice strained with worry as he watches the nurse wheel his bride away briskly. The chair's wheels bounce over cracks in the sidewalk, sending jolts of pain through her body. But she grits her teeth and bears it, grateful for the swift transportation to safety.

Blake screeches into the nearest parking spot, slamming on the brakes with a jolt. He practically sprints towards the hospital, his heart pounding in his chest, the stone in his pocket bouncing against his thigh. Ever since his mother's death, he has been painfully meticulous with every word and thought that crosses his mind, fearing any slip-up could have disastrous consequences, and he can't go through that again.

"Please, please, please, I wish for a safe and healthy delivery of our baby and for Katarina," he whispers as he runs into the building.

He bursts through the hospital doors, scanning the bustling lobby until he spots Katarina being wheeled into the elevator. With a surge of relief, he catches up to them, his hand finding hers as they rise to the maternity ward.

Once they reach the delivery room, Katarina is quickly settled into a hospital gown, her grip on Blake's hand tightening with each wave of pain. Nurses flutter around her, checking monitors and preparing the room for the imminent arrival of their child.

As contractions intensify, Blake stands by Katarina's side, whispering words of encouragement and love into her ear. The room is filled with a mix of tension and excitement, the air electric with anticipation.

"Babe, is your nose bleeding?" Blake asks as Katarina leans back on the bed.

"Oh, that's nothing. You're going to see so much more blood than that today," the nurse laughs as she quickly wipes Katarina's nose.

The nurse's voice is calm and reassuring as she guides Katarina through the final stages of labor.

And then, in an instant, their baby enters the world. The sound of a newborn's cry fills the room, drawing Blake to tears as he catches sight of their little one for the first time.

"It's a boy," the doctor announces with a smile, placing the baby in Katarina's arms. Overwhelmed with emotion, Katarina cradles their son against her chest, tears streaming down her face.

"Do you have a name picked out for the little guy yet?" the doctor asks.

"Oliver," the new mother replies with a tired smile. She gazes down at her son, marveling at his tiny fingers and delicate features. He's perfect in every way. The name "Oliver" seems to fit him perfectly.

"Oliver," Blake repeats softly, testing out the name on his lips. It just sounds right, like it was meant to be. "Welcome to the world, buddy," he whispers, gently touching his son's tiny hand.

Blake leans in to gently kiss Katarina on the forehead, his heart swelling with love and awe at the sight of his newborn son.

"You did great, baby," Blake says lovingly.

Silence.

Blake's frantic gaze falls upon Katarina, and he yells for the nurse, his heart pounding with fear. "She isn't responding? Is she breathing?

The nurses frantically enter the room, pushing Blake aside in their urgency to tend to her. He stands back, watching the madness unfold. Frozen. They quickly check her vitals and find that they are very weak.

In an attempt to bring her back to life, they grab the defibrillator and begin administering shocks. After several attempts, her body finally stirs, and they are able to stabilize her. But the danger is not yet over.

Hours pass as Katarina is closely monitored. She slowly regains consciousness. She is still very weak and frail. However, she is begging for her baby.

Finally, when the doctor clears her, a nurse brings Oliver back into the room. As he is placed in her arms, his cries start to soften as he nuzzles against her warmth and familiar scent.

In the peaceful stillness that follows, Blake's hand reaches out to gently caress Oliver's tiny fingers, overwhelmed with wonder at the miracle of life. He looks at Katarina with a renewed sense of gratitude and love, thankful that she has been brought back from the brink of death.

As they bask in the glow of parenthood, surrounded by the gentle hum of the hospital room, Blake can't help but relish in the deep sense of contentment settling within him.

The room is filled with a sense of peace and serenity as if time itself has slowed down to allow them to savor this precious moment. Blake's gaze shifts from Katarina to Oliver, taking in every detail of his son's face as if trying to memorize it forever.

Oliver's small hand grasps Blake's finger. His grip is surprisingly strong for such a tiny being. This gesture tugs at Blake's heartstrings, filling him with a profound sense of responsibility and love for this little life that now depends on him.

And as the sunset filters through the window, casting a warm glow over the room, Blake makes a silent promise to his newborn son. A promise to be there for him, to protect him, and to love him unconditionally for all the days of his life. No matter what.

In the days and weeks following Oliver's arrival, Blake fully embraces his role as a father with pure joy. The late-night feedings and diaper changes are not mundane tasks, but cherished moments that he treasures with his son.

Blake's heart swells with an indescribable love for his little family as he watches Oliver grow and thrive. However, in the quiet hours of the night, when he's feeding Oliver or sitting alone in the darkness, Blake entertains the ideas and tugs of his darker impulses. Despite his efforts to bury them deep within him, that part of him remains restless, yearning to be unleashed.

The passing of time only seems to intensify these urges, and Blake finds himself struggling more and more to resist them. He knows that he has to keep them hidden for the sake of his newfound happiness and the safety of his wife and son. But sometimes, in the stillness of the night, it's hard not to listen to the seductive whispers of his dark side calling out to him.

One night, as the moon hangs high in the sky, casting a glow through the window of Oliver's nursery, Blake finds himself standing over his son's crib, watching the rise and fall of his chest as he sleeps peacefully. A wave of conflicting emotions is washing over him—overwhelming love for his son mingled with a persistent darkness that lurks within. Not to hurt his son, no, but anyone else outside his little family is fair game.

Without realizing it, he begins tracing a finger along the edge of Oliver's crib, his mind consumed by thoughts he dare not speak aloud. The memory of his mother's death haunts him like a ghost, a constant reminder of the power his darker impulses held over him. But since the wish he made to get rid of his crippling guilt, he has not once felt guilty or remorse for what he had done.

Oliver's sudden cry breaks through his stupor, snapping him back to reality. Blake scoops up his son, cradling him in his arms as he whispers soothing words into the darkness. But even in that tender moment, a voice in the back of his mind whispers temptations that make his heart race with fear.

He quickly shakes off the unsettling thoughts, focusing on Oliver's warmth in his arms and the pure innocence reflected in his son's adorable little face. With a deep breath, he carries

Oliver back to his crib, tucking him in gently. As he watches his son drift back into a peaceful slumber, a surge of protectiveness washes over Blake.

DETERMINED to push aside the shadows that linger at the edge of his consciousness, Blake vows to be the father that Oliver deserves. He promises to shield his family from any harm, even that which may come from within him. With resolute determination, he swears to keep his darker impulses buried deep, locked away where they can never endanger the ones he loves.

15

CHAPTER FIFTEEN

At the tender age of four, Oliver's mischievous and deviant nature has already taken root. Blake constantly notices his frustration rising as he tries to keep up with his rambunctious son. The child seems to have an endless supply of energy and a knack for getting into trouble. More often than not, Blake finds himself exasperated and even angry with his little boy, who always seems to be one step ahead of him.

Blake trudges home after a grueling day at work, hoping for a moment of peace and quiet. But as soon as he steps inside, chaos greets him like an uninvited guest. The kitchen is a complete disaster, with flour covering every surface and tiny footprints leading to a figure standing in the doorway.

Fury boils inside Blake as he takes in the mess, his exhaustion pushed aside by raw anger. He clenches his fists, trying to control the urge to unleash his wrath on the pint-sized culprit. But something snaps inside him when he sees his son Oliver beaming with pride over the destruction.

"Daddy, look what I did!" Oliver exclaims, pointing to the flour-covered floor like it's a masterpiece.

"Katarina!" Blake shrieks, slamming the door behind him. "What the hell is this mess? Why weren't you watching him!"

Katarina, now very thin and frail from an unknown ailment that doctors have not been able to diagnose, slowly walks into the kitchen. Her expression turns to shock and alarm at the scene before her. She glances from the mess to Blake's furious expression.

"I'm so sorry, babe," she says, slowly kneeling down to Oliver's side to clean him up. "He must have gotten into the flour while I was on the phone with my mom. It happened so fast."

But Blake's anger simmers just beneath the surface, threatening to boil over. He watches as Katarina wipes flour off Oliver, his mouth shut tight, struggling to contain his frustration.

"Sorry isn't good enough, Katarina," he snaps, his tone harsh and unforgiving. "You should know better than to leave him unsupervised like this."

"I said I was sorry, Blake," she retorts, her voice tinged with anger. "I can't be with him every second of the day. You've run off every nanny. What do you expect me to do?"

Blake becomes even more angry at her defiance, his temper flaring as he struggles to control his emotions. The tension in the room is thick and palpable as neither of them backs down from the looming confrontation.

Sensing the shift in the atmosphere, Oliver begins to whimper softly in Katarina's arms, looking confused as he turns between his parents.

"Just get the mess cleaned up," he barks, turning away to leave.

"What's happened to you?" she asks.

Blake pauses a moment before continuing to walk away.

However, as he approaches the doorway, something catches his attention, and he turns back to look at the dining room table. A surge of anger overcomes him as he sees a lifeless squirrel, without its head, lying on the table as if on display.

A surge of violent anger courses through Blake's veins, his patience shattering like thin ice. "Oliver, this is NOT okay," he growls through gritted teeth, his voice dripping with venomous irritation. Katarina storms into view, her face twisted in fury. "No sir, you will not speak to our child like that!" she barks ferociously.

"Fucking hell, he's not a baby!" Blake snaps back, his rage now fully unleashed. "And don't you find this situation disturbing? Our kid is a damn psychopath."

"Don't you dare say things like that, Blake!" Katarina screams back, her own anger rising to match his.

"Babe, there is a bloody carcass on the kitchen table!" Blake bellows, his hands shaking with uncontrollable fury. "What other four-year-old in the world would do something so insanely grotesque? And how the fuck did he even manage to do it?"

"Don't you dare say things like that, Blake!" Katarina shouts, her voice trembling with a mix of anger and fear. "He's just a child. He doesn't know any better."

"Know any better? Are you kidding me? He shouldn't KNOW how to do that!" he growls through gritted teeth, walking out of the room, "This kid needs help!"

Blake paces back and forth in the living room, his mind racing with a whirlwind of emotions. He can't shake off the image of the lifeless squirrel on the table. The realization that his son might have more dark in him than even he does sends a chill down his spine.

As he tries to collect his thoughts, Katarina enters the

room, her expression softening as she approaches him. "Blake, we need to talk about this," she begins, her voice gentle yet firm.

"Ya think?" he snaps back. "Seriously, Katarina, you can't defend that! That is insane. He's four! Speaking of, where is he?"

"Calm down," she pleads, her voice shaking with fear. "He's just playing in the bathtub with shaving cream. There's barely any water in there."

"And what about the...the table?"

"I wrapped up the entire tablecloth into a ball and put it in a trash bag and threw it in the can outside," her voice quivers; she's never been so afraid of Blake before.

"I'm going to go and talk to him," Blake says as he strides past Katarina.

"No, he's just a little boy; you're too angry. You're going to terrify him!" Katarina pleads.

"Perfect, that's exactly what I want. He needs to be paralyzed with fear. Why aren't you more upset or disgusted?"

As he approaches the cracked open door, the sounds of splashing and giggles filter out. He pushes open the door to find Oliver standing in the tub, grinning widely as he smears shaving cream all over his face.

"Daddy! Look what I can do!" Oliver exclaims, his innocent tone at odds with the queasyness churning in Blake's stomach.

Trying to hide his turmoil from his son, Blake forces a smile and kneels beside the bathtub. "That's great, buddy," he says, his voice strained. "But let's clean up now, okay? Daddy needs to have a talk with you."

As Blake helps him out of the tub and wraps him in a towel, he can't help but notice how small and fragile his son looks at that moment.

Leading Oliver to his room, Blake gets him dressed and

settles him on the bed, sitting down beside him. He takes a deep breath, trying to find the right words to address the disturbing events of the day without losing his cool again.

"Oliver," he begins, his voice soft yet serious, "what you did today was not okay. Can you tell me why you thought it was a good idea to...hurt that squirrel?"

Oliver's eyes widen with innocence as he looks up at his father, his face devoid of any guilt or shame. "I wanted to see how it felt," he says simply, his voice filled with curiosity.

A chill runs down Blake's spine at the matter-of-fact way his son speaks.

"To feel what it's like to kill something?" Blake asks, his voice barely holding it together.

Oliver nods solemnly, his small face a mixture of confusion and sincerity. "Yes," he whispers.

The realization hit him like a bolt of lightning. The darkness he has in himself, the darkness he has fought so hard to keep at bay for the last several years, is also in his son.

Blake's heart pounds in his chest as he looks at Oliver with a mix of shock and disgust. He finally musters the courage to ask, "And how did it make you feel?"

Oliver's innocent smile sends a chill down his spine as he replies, "I liked it."

Blake stands there astonished. He can't believe what he just heard. He begins to wonder if this is some sort of sick, curious phase or a twisted punishment from God that he will now have to endure.

As the months pass, Oliver's reckless and dangerous behavior continues to push Blake to his breaking point. He dreads coming home, expecting to find more dead animals or worse. Every moment Blake spends with Oliver is spent in a state of heightened alertness, constantly scanning for any signs of disturbing behavior from the unpredictable young boy who seems to delight in causing chaos and fear.

As much as he tries to suppress it, the urge to use the stone still lingers in the back of Blake's mind. It taunts him in moments of frustration and anger, whispering enticing promises of a quick solution. Despite his efforts to stay in control, he recognizes himself slipping further into the grasp of the stone's alluring power. The temptation pulls him towards an action he knows he will regret—tempting him with false promises and temporary relief that could only lead to disastrous consequences.

Early one morning, in a moment of weakness, Blake goes into a shoebox in the closet and pulls out the smooth, cool stone. With trembling hands, he closes his eyes, and to avoid mixing up his thoughts, he whispers a wish into the air. "I wish...."

But before he can finish his sentence, a small voice interrupts him. "Daddy, what are you doing?" Oliver questions, his footsteps softly padding against the floor as he enters the kitchen.

"Ugh, nothing, kiddo," Blake sighs, running his hands through his hair as he stares out the window. "Just thinking about the endless tasks waiting for me at the office today." He turns to his son, who is now sitting across from him at the kitchen table. "Do me a favor and try to act like a normal kid today, okay?"

Katarina bursts into the room, her face flushed with anger, trying to catch her breath. "Blake!" she exclaims.

"Babe, I'm serious," Blake says, gesturing towards their son. "You need to get this kid checked out by a shrink. He's just not right."

Katarina is in shock. Through her wheezing, she says, "We're going to have a serious talk about this tonight." Her eyes narrow as she looks at her husband. "And maybe you're the one who needs to see a shrink. You act like you hate our son! You think he doesn't notice?"

"Stop being so dramatic! I don't hate our son," Blake protests defensively. "I just hate how... weird he is. It's embarrassing and sometimes straight disturbing."

Katarina shakes her head in disappointment. "Nice, real nice," she mutters sarcastically. "You know what? Just go to the office."

"Gladly," Blake retorts, annoyed. "Now the little brat has me fighting with you!"

As Blake storms out of the house, his anger and frustration boiling over, he can't help but think that things are spiraling out of control. As he drives to work, his thoughts are consumed by the growing darkness within him, the stone's whispers echoing in his mind.

Arriving at the office, Blake tries to escape the chaos at home. He leans back in his chair and runs his hands through his hair, trying to block out the voices in his head.

The sound of footsteps echoes down the hallway, and Blake's head snaps up, his eyes narrowing as he spots Taylor glaring at him from the open doorway. A wave of tension and awkwardness radiates off her, a constant reminder of their disastrous night together. But Blake remains unfazed, his indifference to her obvious.

"Jackass," she mutters venomously under her breath.

A smirk tugs at the corner of Blake's lips as he responds, "Oh, Taylor, Taylor. You don't want to piss me off again, do you?"

She flips him off and storms away down the hall, seething with anger.

Chuckling darkly to himself, Blake mutters, "I didn't think so."

A knock on the door startles him. Blake looks up again to see his boss standing in the doorway with a concerned expression etched on his face.

"Hey, Blake. Is everything okay?" he questions, eyebrow arched in concern.

Blake forces a smile, trying to appear composed despite the storm raging inside him. "Yeah, just dealing with some family stuff. You know how it is."

Mr. Hayes steps into the office and closes the door behind him, his expression serious. "I've known you for a long time, Blake. And I can see that something is really bothering you. You're a good employee, one of the best I've ever had. But lately, your work has been suffering."

Blake's voice rises, his frustration and anger bubbling to the surface. He stands up abruptly, causing his boss to take a step back in surprise. "I work harder than anyone at this company!" he exclaims, his hands clenching into fists at his sides.

Mr. Hayes raises a hand in a placating gesture. "I know you do, Blake. You've always been dedicated and hardworking. But something has changed recently. Your mind seems elsewhere, and it's affecting your performance. I came in here because I needed you to cover another meeting this afternoon, but now I'm not sure you can even handle it. I need you to pull it together, Blake," Mr. Hayes says firmly. "Your personal issues are affecting your job at this point, and I can't have that. Forget about the meeting; I'll have Axel cover it."

The anger that's been building up for weeks, months, or maybe even years has reached the surface. As Blake stands there glaring at his boss, he makes a decision. He can't take it anymore - the constant arguing with Katarina, the frustration with Oliver, and the never-ending expectations at work. The whispers of the stone grow louder in his mind, promising a release from his pain, and he can't ignore them anymore.

"It's really not a good idea to fuck with me right now," Blake says.

"Excuse me. Is that a threat!?"

Blake's fists are balled up tightly and ready to strike. "Mr. Hayes, get the fuck out of my office before I.."

"Before you, what exactly? Mr. Hayes questions, scrutinizing his employee carefully. "Blake, what in the world are you doing? Are you having a nervous breakdown? I'm calling security. You need to leave this building now!"

"MR. HAYES, get out of my office!" Blake yells.

"Blake, I don't know who you think you are or what you're doing, but you're fired! You have five minutes to get outta this building with your stuff and your dignity before I have security throw you out!"

Blake lowers his head, taking a deep breath, and then another. Mr. Hayes stands in front of him, lost in confusion when Blake slowly raises his head and has a creepy smile plastered on his face. "You should've left when you had the chance. Now it's too late."

"What in the...?" Mr. Hayes begins before gripping his chest and doubling over in pain. His face contorts, and his eyes widen as he struggles to breathe.

Blake kneels down and runs a shaky hand through his hair.

"What's that? I can't understand you," Blake whispers, glancing around to make sure none of the other employees are nearby to offer assistance.

Mr. Hayes drops to the floor, groaning and clutching at his chest. Beads of sweat form on his forehead and trickle down his face as he battles through the agony.

"Oh no, someone get help," Blake continues to whisper, a

twisted smirk of malice spreading across his face like a venomous snake. Watching Mr. Hayes writhe in agony with sadistic pleasure.

Thirty seconds pass, and Blake no longer hears Mr. Hayes struggling. Deciding to check for a pulse and finding none, he nods with a sense of approval and shouts in pretend urgency.

"Help! We need help, quickly!"

In a matter of seconds, chaos consumes his office as people dart around frantically, their panicked screams ringing out across the building. Tears streak down some faces while others try effortlessly to revive their beloved boss. Yet amidst the mayhem, Blake stands still with absolutely no expression on his face. But internally, he is reveling in the hysteria, relishing in the fear and confusion of those around him.

As the paramedics file into the office, he watches them attend to Mr. Hayes with a smirk on his face, a thrill of satisfaction at the sight of their desperation and panic.

In the midst of the chaos, Blake's mind becomes clearer than it's been in weeks. His thoughts are focused and precise, and his actions are calculated and deliberate. He has power and is never going back to being weak or out of control again.

16

CHAPTER SIXTEEN

Though Blake's conscience nags at him, the power and exhilaration from his actions are undeniable. The stone has granted his wish in a twisted way he never could have predicted, but it makes him feel invincible once again. As he arrives home that evening, Katarina's concerned expression can't be denied. "Blake, I heard about what happened at your office this afternoon; why didn't you call me?" she said worriedly, scanning his face for a sign of how he was coping.

"It actually happened in my office," Blake finally said. "It was a horrible tragedy. But there's nothing that can be done about it now."

As Katarina studies him for a moment longer, she can't help but notice something different about him. His usually confident demeanor seems to have shifted, replaced by a sense of detachment. "Are you okay, Blake?" she asked with genuine concern. "You seem...different."

"I wish people would quit..."

Blake gathers his composure, forcing a reassuring smile, and continues, "I'm fine; don't worry about me."

Blake slowly scans over his wife's features; he can see the unease in her eyes and the subtle tension on her face. Despite his love for her, he can't bring himself to let go of the power that consumes him. And in this moment, he can't help but relish in a sense of twisted joy. "I just need some time to myself, okay?" he says, his voice cold and distant. Katarina's shoulders slump as she's filled with concern. Blake turns on his heel and disappears into the house, leaving her standing alone in the entryway.

"Blake, please talk to me," she calls after him, her voice trembling slightly.

But Blake doesn't turn back. As he walks down the dimly lit hallway, the stone in his pocket seems to pulse with a life of its own, whispering promises of even greater strength and dominance. In this moment, Blake has never felt more alive.

As he reaches his office, he locks the door behind him and sinks into the plush armchair by the bookcase.

The sound of a knock on the door startles him out of his thoughts. Katarina's voice filters through the wood, filled with concern. "Blake, please open the door. We need to talk. You shouldn't be holding this stuff inside. Let me help you."

"Katarina, please. I just want to be alone for a little while. Why can't you understand that?"

Katarina begins to sob quietly as she backs away from the door. The sound of her footsteps fading away down the hall, leaving Blake alone in the dimly lit room.

With a heavy sigh, he rises from the armchair and paces the room, the stone in his pocket growing heavier with each step. It's clear what he wants and what he needs. He makes a silent wish to be a powerful man. He sees how people in fancy suits in meetings he's been a part of or even walking down the street are treated and wants to experience that. The stone pulsates in his pocket, and he knows that the stone has granted yet another wish.

Later that night as he's about to slip into bed and finally get some rest, his phone rings. Katarina turns to her husband curiously as she crawls into bed next to him.

"Who in the world is calling you at this hour?" she asks, her voice muffled by the comforter she's pulled up past her chin.

Blake shrugs, picking up the phone. He answers with a tentative "Hello?"

"Blake, it's Daniel from the board of trustees. I'm sorry for calling so late. I know today must have been tough for you. So my first question is, how are you holding up?"

"Oh, um, I'm fine. But thank you for asking."

"Absolutely. If there is anything you need, please don't hesitate to contact a member of the board. We are here to support you and the rest of the staff in any way we can during this time, which brings me to the second reason for my call. We just concluded an emergency meeting, and after a unanimous vote, we all agreed that you should take on the role of VP if you are willing.

"Are you serious?" Blake shouts, his voice filled with excitement and disbelief.

"I didn't want to wait until tomorrow to let you know, and I'm boarding a plane in a few minutes, so I don't have much time. I want you to be ready for what will hit you tomorrow. Christina is well aware of all the meetings lined up for the day, and there shouldn't be anything you can't handle. We're fairly certain it'll be a seamless transition for you." Daniel says confidently.

His sudden outburst causes Katarina to sit up straight in

bed, her curiosity piqued. She eagerly waits for him to explain, her mind racing with questions.

"What is it? What's going on? Who is it?" she whispers rapidly, unable to contain her anticipation.

But Blake waves her off and raises his finger, indicating he will share the news in just a minute.

"Thank you, sir. I'll be sure not to disappoint you or any of the other members." The words taste like bile in Blake's mouth, his mind flashing back to all the times he had uttered the same promise to Mr. Hayes. But this time, it's different.

As he hangs up the phone, a grin spreads across his face. "Katarina, did you hear that? I'm the new VP." He doesn't even hear her response; instead, his mind races with thoughts of what he can achieve now that he holds such a prestigious position.

"Who can stop me now," he mumbles as he lays his head on his pillow.

"What did you say?" Katarina questions, snuggling up next to her husband.

Blake lets out a chuckle, dismissing Katarina's question. "Oh, nothing important. Just thinking out loud, you know?" His mind, however, is far from quiet.

Visions of power and control dance through his mind. He finds himself in an unending circle, chasing an insatiable desire for more. That evening, he finally falls into a deep and restful slumber, the best he's experienced in years.

Blake's mind is on overdrive the following day as he heads to work. He spots a construction crew working on the side of the road. His curiosity turns to malice as he watches them, fueled by the pulsating energy emanating from the mysterious stone in his pocket. He whispers a dark wish for one of the workers to take three giant steps backward and smirks as he sees the man walk mindlessly into oncoming traffic through his rearview mirror. The sound of screeching brakes and shattering glass fills his ears as chaos erupts behind him.

Satisfied with the chaos he caused, Blake pulls into the parking lot of his office building with a wicked chuckle. "Glad that happened behind me, or else I would've been late," he mutters with a grin, relishing in the thought of avoiding the ensuing traffic jam caused by his actions.

As soon as he enters the front door, a group of solemn employees loom before him, shattering the jolly mood he had been basking in just moments before.

As he confidently strides through the office, the employees part like a sea before him. The air is thick and filled with a mix of fear and apprehension. The sound of hushed whispers and darting glances follow in his wake.

At last, he reaches his new office at the end of the hallway - a grand space befitting a Vice President. The high ceilings and floor-to-ceiling windows give an expansive view of the cityscape beyond. Blake takes a seat behind the imposing desk, recognizing every bit of the influential leader he has become.

The smooth stone hums with energy in his pocket, a constant reminder of the control and influence now at his fingertips. A twisted smile plays on his lips as he gazes out at the city.

Christina sits diligently at her desk in the far corner of his spacious office. As Mr. Hayes' former trusted assistant, she has been assigned to Blake since he took over the CEO position.

"Is there anything I can help you with this morning, Blake?" The smell of freshly brewed coffee wafts through the air as she nervously shifts her weight from foot to foot, waiting for his response.

Blake hesitates for a moment before speaking, a sly smirk on his face. "Actually, Christina, thank you for asking. I could use a cup of that coffee I smell right about now." He leans back in his chair and crosses one leg over the other, a casual posture meant to convey power and confidence.

As Christina turns to leave, she hesitates for a moment before mustering up the courage to speak. "Mr. Hayes always spoke highly of you. I'm sure you'll do great things as the new VP."

"Why, Christina," he says with a slight hint of surprise. Honestly, it was unexpected for her or anyone in the office to say something so kind, and he wasn't quite sure how to respond. The corners of his mouth tugged upwards into a small smile as he searched for the right words. "What a kind thing for you to say. Thank you."

Blake watches as Christina scurries out of the office on her way to get his coffee. He leans back in his chair, reveling in the insatiable desire for more control over every aspect of his life. The city outside his window buzzes with life. Blake gets up from his seat and makes his way to the window.

He presses his palms against the cool window and gazes out at the city, his thoughts a swirling mess. He can hear the clanking of Christina's heels against the tile floor as she makes her way back to his office. He squints and watches for her reflection in the glass as he has a disturbing thought.

Within seconds, Christina stumbles through the door carrying a steaming cup of coffee. Instantly, she's on her knees, the hot liquid cascading down her body as Blake watches with amusement.

Christina lets out a pained cry as the scalding hot coffee seeps through her clothes, leaving red welts on her skin. Her hands shake uncontrollably as she tries to wipe away the steaming liquid, tears welling up in her eyes from both the physical pain and the humiliation of her clumsy accident in front of the new VP.

Blake's grin widens as he watches her distress, relishing

the power his wish has given him. "Oh dear, it seems we've had a little mishap," he says with faux concern, though deep inside, he is filled with a cruel satisfaction. Why don't you run to the bathroom and clean yourself up?"

Christina, her face red from embarrassment and pain, nods and scurries out of the room, leaving Blake alone once more in his office.

He returns to the window and watches the city bustling below him, coming to life as the workday begins. The streets are filled with cars and people rushing to their destinations while the buildings stretch up towards the sky. His gaze lingers on a group of construction workers on top of the building across the street, their bright yellow helmets standing out against the gray roof. They look more like ants, moving about with purpose, precision, and efficiency. He takes in the scene for several minutes, marveling at the organized chaos.

One worker in particular, a man whose body language is tense and agitated, catches Blake's attention. His arms flail wildly as he seemingly shouts at his co-worker, his face contorted with anger and frustration.

"Here you are, sir."

Another assistant brings in Blake's coffee.

"Why thank you," he says.

Blake picks up the hot coffee, looks towards the building, and has a thought.

With a sudden jolt, the worker loses his footing on the unstable rooftop and begins to teeter dangerously over the edge. The other workers on the roof freeze, their faces a mixture of shock and horror as they watch their co-worker lose his balance.

The man's face twists into a grimace of fear and anger as he reaches desperately for something to grab onto, but it's too late. He tumbles backward off the roof, his body arching mid-air as he plummets toward the cold, hard ground below.

Blake watches with detached curiosity as the man falls, watching it all unfold before him like a gruesome slow-motion movie. He knows what's coming next but can't help but watch and wait.

He was so transfixed on the scene before him he didn't hear Christina walk up behind him until she let out a blood-curdling scream. Blake jumps in surprise, whirling around to face the source of the noise. Christina stands there, her hands cupped over her mouth, eyes wide with terror as she stares at him, her chest heaving.

"Oh my God," she breathed, her voice shaking. "That man... did you... did you see that?"

Blake looks down at the man's lifeless body crumpled on the pavement and yawns as if it doesn't phase him. The other workers on the roof are frozen in shock and disbelief, their faces pale and stricken.

Blake, showing no emotion and jumping back in stride, said, "Christina, I'm going to need Mr. Hayes's notes for the upcoming ten-thirty appointment. Thanks"

Christina steps back, fear and horror consuming her from head to toe. "I... I can't believe that just happened right there. In front of us."

The sound of hurried footsteps and panicked voices fills the office as people come sprinting from all corners of the building. Their faces are etched with worry and confusion as they look between Blake and Christina.

"What's going on? Why are you screaming?" they demand.

Christina can barely choke out an answer, her voice trembling with shock and fear. "That man... he fell off the building," she stammers, tears streaming down her face uncontrollably.

The atmosphere in the room shifts from confusion to chaos

as everyone tries to process the shocking news. But Blake's annoyance cuts through it all. He barks out a demand: "Can someone please take her out of my office? And the rest of you get to work!"

The commotion in the office seems to slowly die out as Blake's callous words hang in the air. Still reeling from the traumatic sight she just witnessed, Christina is ushered out of the room by a kind colleague who gently holds her shoulder. Tears continue to flow freely down her cheeks as she is led away from the scene, her mind overwhelmed by a mix of horror and disbelief.

Meanwhile, Blake remains in his office, a mask of cold indifference firmly in place as he watches the emergency responders arrive at the scene below. A knock at his door interrupts his thoughts. Without waiting for a response, Axel enters the office.

"What the hell are you doing in here?" Blake demands.

"There's a doctor on line one for you from Grace Memorial Hospital. They said it's about your wife."

17

CHAPTER SEVENTEEN

Blake's heart skips a beat. The mere mention of the hospital and his beloved wife sends a shockwave through his body. Without hesitation, he snatches up the phone, his hands trembling with worry. His ordinarily calm demeanor is replaced with sheer panic as he answers the call.

"This is Blake. What's happened?" his voice cracks with emotion.

The caller on the other end relays the devastating news in hushed tones, each word like a physical blow to Blake's chest. "Your wife, Katarina, is in critical condition. The doctors are unsure what's wrong with her. You need to come now."

As soon as he hears the news, Blake's mind goes blank. He stumbles backward and grabs onto the edge of his desk to keep from falling. His breathing becomes shallow and rapid as he tries to process what he just heard. Without even thinking, he snatches his coat off the back of his chair, knocking over a stack of papers in his haste, and sprints out of the office, leaving Axel behind in a state of confusion and fear.

Blake's car screeches to a halt outside the hospital, the

tires kicking up a cloud of dust. He jumps out without bothering to shut the door, his heart pounding in his chest.

As soon as he enters the hospital, the familiar sterile smell hits him in the face. The sound of beeping machinery and muted conversations fill his ears as he races through the halls. He stops at a nursing station and frantically demands, "Where's my wife?"

The nurse calmly and kindly directs Blake to a private room. Blake frantically pushes through the door, his fear and panic clearly evident in his usual poised posture.

There she is, lying in bed, pale and fragile-looking. Her breathing is labored, and she looks like she's in immense pain.

Her eyes flutter open, meeting his gaze briefly before closing again. The machine beside her beeps in a steady rhythm, each sound piercing Blake's heart.

He reaches out, taking her hand and flinching at the chill of clammy sweat that has started to coat her skin. His heart breaks at the sight of her.

Tears well up, and a lump forms in his throat as he watches Katarina lying there, so vulnerable and fragile. He leans in close, gently kissing her forehead, whispering words of love and reassurance into her ear.

"Katarina, my love," he murmurs, his voice thick with emotion. "I'm here."

She stirs faintly at his touch, a soft moan escaping her lips. Her eyelids flutter open once more. Weakly, she whispers, "Blake... I'm scared."

The harsh reality of the situation hits him like a ton of bricks as he watches the love of his life struggle for each breath.

"I'm begging you, Blake, look after Oliver. Don't be so harsh with him. He's just a child, your child," she pleads, the words coming out in gasps as she fights to speak.

"Don't do that, baby, you're not going anywhere. The doctors are going to figure this out, and you're going to be better than ever. Please, babe, I don't want to do this without you."

The sound of monitors beeping in the background creates a haunting backdrop to their conversation. The tension in the room is palpable as Blake refuses to let go of Katarina's hand as if holding on tight enough could somehow keep her anchored to this world.

Hours pass in agonizing uncertainty, the doctors coming in and out of the room with furrowed brows and murmured discussions. Each moment passes like an eternity, filling him with dread.

Finally, a senior doctor enters the room with a grave expression, making Blake's heart sink.

"May we speak outside?" asks the doctor.

Blake nods and follows the doctor out of the room, leaving Katarina to rest.

"Do you have any news?" Blake asks, the desperation evident in his voice.

"Yes, but I'm afraid it isn't good news. I'm sorry to have to be the one to inform you, but despite our best efforts, your wife's condition is continuing to deteriorate.

"Please, there must be something else you can do: another treatment, a new specialist, something, anything. I'm begging you," Blake pleads.

The doctor pauses, his expression softening slightly at the raw anguish on Blake's face. He places a hand on Blake's shoulder, offering what little solace he can in such a heartbreaking moment.

"I know this is incredibly difficult to hear, but we have exhausted all possible options. Katarina's body is simply too weak to fight any longer," the doctor states gently, his voice filled with empathy.

Blinking back tears, Blake walks back into the room and leans into Katarina, his voice cracking. "I love you so much, Katarina. You are my everything." He kisses her forehead and lets his lips linger for a few extra minutes. Taking in her scent.

As the hours tick by, Katarina's breathing becomes increasingly shallow.

The doctor watches him with a mixture of sympathy and respect, knowing that this man is facing one of life's greatest challenges - losing the love of his life.

The room grows quiet, save for the sound of Katarina's labored breaths and the beeping of the machines. Blake holds her hand tightly, focusing every ounce of strength on keeping it from slipping out of his grasp.

The door creaks open, and Blake's dad walks in, carrying Oliver. He cautiously approaches the bed.

"I thought they should get to say goodbye."

"Dad, he shouldn't see her like this," Blake begins, but Oliver practically dives out of his grandfather's arms, trying to get to his mother.

"Mommy!"

Katarina offers a faint smile when she sees her son. She reaches out with her free hand, her weak grasp just enough to touch Oliver's cheek. "My brave, big, handsome boy," she whispers, her voice barely audible over the sound of the machines and her labored breathing.

"Tell Mommy you love her," Blake says more sternly than he meant to.

"I love you, Mommy." Oliver echoes back, his voice filled with confusion and worry. He turns to his father and asks, "Daddy, what's wrong with Mommy?"

Blake lets out a frustrated sigh.

"Dad, please take Oliver and go home," Blake pleads, pushing the young boy into his grandfather's arms and leading them toward the door.

Oliver's cries grow louder as he resists, wanting to stay with his mother despite the tension in the room. "No, I want to stay with mommy!" he wails.

"Go with grandpa, son," Blake said firmly, trying to soothe his son. "Be good."

As they leave, the sound of Oliver's cries echoes through the hallway, a heartbreaking reminder of the current situation.

Hours turn into days as Blake keeps vigil by Katarina's bedside. She has slipped out of consciousness, so he spends his time praying and wishing for her to wake up and return to him. The only constant is her labored breathing and continuous nose bleeding.

"Baby, please! You have to wake up. I just wish you would say my name and tell me you love me. Hell, I would take you yelling at me. Just wake up."

Blake leans in to kiss her forehead and feels a warm wetness against his lips. He pulls away to see a tiny red droplet at the tip of her nose. Without warning, the machines beside her bed start beeping frantically before going flatline. Blake gets up in a hurry. His cell phone and the stone fall from his pocket onto the bed. A nurse comes into the room, pushing Blake out into the hallway. He stands outside the room, staring at the closed door in disbelief as chaos erupts behind it.

Minutes later, the doctor emerges from the room with a solemn expression. He can see the doctor's mouth moving, but his words are inaudible. But he knows exactly what he's attempting to tell him.

He just lost the love of his life. Forever.

18

CHAPTER EIGHTEEN

Blake's world instantly shatters into a million pieces as he kneels on the cold hospital floor. Sorrow and disbelief envelop him. Doctors and nurses come past, their voices distant. He can only stare at the door, where, just moments ago, his wife lay dying. The image of her frail body, her final moment, playing on repeat in his mind like a nightmare on loop- the droplet of blood, the flatlining machine, the look on the doctor's face.

An eternity passes before Blake finds the strength to rise up off the floor.

His body is heavy, every movement an effort as he pushes himself up from the cold, sterile hospital floor. As he stands, a wave of dizziness washes over him, and he has to cling to the nearest wall for support. The world around him blurs as grief threatens to consume him whole.

He walks out of the hospital, the world turning surreal and far away. The sunlight is too harsh, and the traffic sounds are too loud. He doesn't know where to go or what to do. His entire being has become hollow, like a part of him has been ripped away forever.

Blake mechanically gets into his car and starts driving aimlessly, the scenery passing by in a blur. Memories of Katarina flood his mind - her laughter, her touch, her love. How can she be gone? How can he live in a world without her?

He continues to drive until the sun has set and the stars are high in the sky. Then, Blake finally finds himself at their favorite spot—a secluded hill overlooking the city. The cool night breeze ruffles his hair, and he gazes at the twinkling lights below.

In the days that follow, Blake finds himself drifting through life in a fog. His mind is consumed with memories of Katarina, their laughter and adventures together captured in photographs that he can't stop looking at.

He hasn't felt close to his son, Oliver, in years. In fact, if he's being honest with himself, he probably hasn't felt love for him since he was an infant. Now, every time he sees him, it's like a knife twisting in his heart, a constant reminder of his loss. All of his happiness is gone. Instead, it's replaced by bitterness and resentment towards a child he no longer wants.

In the years that followed Katarina's death, he would often push Oliver's care off onto his father, using the excuse of work to get out of his fatherly duties. However, after about three years, his father decided that he was ready to go out and live life again. So he moved to Arizona into a gated adult community. Leaving Blake to raise his son alone, and he hated every second of it.

Blake's resentment toward Oliver grows with each passing day, causing him to become a shell of the man he once was. He sees the boy as a constant reminder of the love he has lost, a burden he never wanted to bear. His days are filled with anger and frustration, and he takes it out on the innocent child who looked up to him for love and guidance while ensuring it isn't visible to anyone so as not to draw unwanted attention.

On the other hand, Oliver tried his best to win his father's affection. He would clean the house, make his own meals, and excel in school, hoping to earn a smile or a kind word from Blake. But all he receives in return are harsh words and neglect.

Oliver learned to navigate his father's volatile moods, always walking on eggshells in his presence. Blake would lock his son in his tiny room, consisting of only a twin-size bed, whenever possible. Even the window was nailed shut. However, Oliver sneaks in books and hides them under his mattress. The confinement became a blessing in disguise, shielding him from his father's neglect and anger. But even in his solitude, Oliver clung to the stories in books, finding comfort and escape in the pages that transported him far away from his harsh reality.

The walls of their home echo with silence, broken only by the occasional outburst from Blake directed at Oliver.

The tension in the house grows thicker with each passing day, an invisible barrier separating father and son. Oliver becomes astute at anticipating Blake's moods, learning to avoid him when he senses the storm brewing within his father.

One evening, as darkness covers the house, a loud crash sounds from the living room. Oliver's heart pounds in his chest as he cautiously steps out of his room, fear mingling with curiosity. He finds Blake slumped on the couch, an empty bottle of whiskey at his feet. The room smells of alcohol and sweat.

Oliver hesitates, unsure of what to do. Slowly, he approaches his father and cautiously places a hand on his shoulder. Blake startles at the touch, his head snapping up to meet Oliver's gaze. The father and son simply stare at each other in silence for a moment.

"Go back to your room, Oliver," Blake snaps finally, his voice slurred from the alcohol. His eyes are bloodshot. "I don't want to deal with you right now."

"I can get you some water, Dad," Oliver offers quietly, trying to hide his fear behind a mask of calmness.

"What would make you believe I would want anything from you?"

Oliver flinches at the harshness in his father's tone. "I was just trying to help you, old man!" Instantly regretting what he said, but it was too late.

Blake is instantly angered at Oliver's retort. He pushes himself up from the couch, staggering slightly as he looms over his son. "You ungrateful little brat," he slurs, venom dripping from his words. "I've had it up to here with you."

His hand shoots out and lands a stinging slap across the side of Oliver's face. The room falls silent as the slap echo lingers in the air.

Oliver bites his lip to keep himself from crying. He knows that showing weakness will only enrage his father further. In silence, he turns and retreats to his room, his cheek throbbing from the force of his father's blow.

As Oliver shuts the door behind him, he falls onto his bed, his heart pounding in his chest. The stinging pain on his cheek slowly fades as he buries himself into his covers, more isolated and alone than ever before. He knew better than to talk like that to his father, but sometimes he just gets so angry. He even has horrible dreams at night about the things he would like to do to his dad. But in the morning, when he wakes up, all he can focus on is his mom and what she would think if she knew what he was thinking, and then he is consumed with guilt for having such dark and awful thoughts.

Days turned into weeks and weeks into months. Blake's drinking continues, and his treatment of Oliver grows worse with each passing day. The boy dreads the sound of the front door opening, knowing that it could only mean one thing – his father was home.

In Oliver's small room, a mini-library has grown as he finds solace in the characters on the pages of his beloved books. He finds that he can escape from reality for a while through them. From adventure to mystery, Oliver loses himself in the worlds created by the authors he admires so much.

One evening, as Oliver sat curled up on his bed with his latest book, he heard footsteps coming down the hall. His heart pounded in his chest as his father approached his door. The handle turned, and without warning, Blake burst into his room.

"You believe you're so smart, don't you?" Blake slurs.

"Whatever you're upset about, I'm sorry, Dad," Oliver says quietly, knowing that he can never predict how his father will react. Blake's face twists in anger as he advances towards Oliver, who instinctively backs away.

"You're nothing but a burden to me," Blake spits out, his breath reeking of whiskey. His hand lashes out and grabs Oliver by the collar, shaking him violently.

Oliver reels in shock at his father's statement. While he's always known that's how his father felt about him, hearing it come directly from his mouth is different.

"I..." but before Oliver can finish his thought, Blake shoves him back, sending him crashing against the wall. Pain shoots through Oliver's body as he crumples to the floor, his book falling from his grasp. He curls into a ball, trying to shield himself from his father's blows. Blake stands over him, filled with rage and contempt.

Oliver curls tighter into a ball, his arms shielding his head as he waits for the next blow to fall. His heart pounds in his chest, the taste of blood filling his mouth from where his father's fist had struck.

A spark of defiance ignites within him, pushing aside the consuming dread.

"Mom would be disgusted with you," Oliver whimpers.

Blake's eyes flash with fury as he looms over the boy. His hand whips back once more, and Oliver braces for the impact.

But this time, the blow never lands. Instead, a voice cuts through the silence in the room.

"What the hell is going on in here?"

Oliver's heart leaps as he recognizes the voice. He dares to and sees his grandfather standing in the doorway, his expression a mix of shock and anger.

His father, caught off guard, takes a step back from Oliver. "This is none of your business, Dad," Blake sneers, his voice dripping with hostility. "This is between me and my little shit of a son."

Oliver's grandfather steps further into the room, positioning himself protectively in front of his grandson. His gaze flickers from Blake to Oliver as he takes in the scene before him.

"Watch your damn mouth! That's my grandson you're talking about!

"I said mind your business!" Slurring and wobbling.

"You've made it my business by behaving like a damn fool," he replies firmly. "Did I ever raise a hand to you like this? I didn't raise you to behave this way. "Go take a shower, son. We'll talk about this after you've sobered up."

"You don't tell me what to do in my own house!" Blake snaps back angrily.

"Your house? Who built this house? This was mine and your mother's long before you were even born," his father spat, pointing a finger at him. "Don't you dare talk to me about this house. Now get outta here before I drag you out myself."

Blake takes a step forward, squaring up to his dad. Nose to nose. "Really? He scoffs. YOU? You're going to drag me out, huh?" he challenges.

"Just go to bed, son; you're going to realize you're being a jackass in the morning!" His dad shoots daggers at him, piercing into his soul. He's always had a deep, profound respect for his dad for his entire life. Therefore, he knew he must be careful with his words and thoughts. Taking a deep breath, he turns his head and mutters a quiet "Yes sir." before storming out of the room and slamming the door behind him.

The walls shake, and Oliver and his grandpa exchange a look of shock. Oliver's grandfather turns to him, his expression softening as he kneels beside the trembling young man. "Are you okay, Oliver?" he asks gently, reaching out to help him get back to his feet.

Oliver nods shakily, accepting his grandfather's hand and allowing himself to be helped up. "Thank you, Grandpa. I've missed you."

"I've missed you too, buddy," he says, enveloping him in a warm hug. "Listen, I'll talk to your dad about what just happened in here. I know he didn't mean it. He's just going through a tough time right now. That's not who he really is."

Oliver lets out a deep, weary sigh as he looks up at his grandpa. The older man stands tall and strong despite his age, radiating a sense of calm and reassurance. "Grandpa," Oliver begins.

"Now, now," his Grandpa replies with a gentle smile. Don't worry. Everything will be okay." His voice is like a warm blanket, wrapping around Oliver's worries and fears and soothing them away.

As they stand in the quiet room, Oliver realizes how much

he has missed having his grandfather around. Memories of their fishing trips, shared laughter, and wisdom imparted flood back to him, reminding him of their bond.

"Alright, kiddo, why don't you get some sleep? Tomorrow is a new day," his grandfather says while patting him on the back and heading toward the door. "I'll take you to school in the morning. Give your dad a break."

Oliver nods gratefully and watches his grandfather leave the room, closing the door behind him. Alone in his room once again, Oliver takes a deep breath and looks around the room. As he climbs into bed, he picks up his book from the floor and rubs his fingers over the bent cover. Opening it to where he left off, he immerses himself in the world of adventure and mystery.

The next morning, as he gets ready for school, Oliver hears muffled movements in the kitchen, signaling that his grandfather is already up. Oliver makes his way to the kitchen, where his grandfather sits at the table, sipping a cup of coffee.

"Morning, kiddo," his grandfather greets him warmly. "Sleep okay?"

Oliver nods, mustering a small smile in return. "Yeah, thanks, Grandpa."

After a breakfast of pancakes and syrup, Oliver grabs his backpack and heads for the front door, where his grandfather is waiting.

"Listen, Oliver," he begins, placing a hand on the young boy's shoulder. "I want you to know that I talked to your dad this morning before he left for work. He's sorry for what happened. You have to understand that your dad is going through a rough time. That doesn't excuse his behavior, but we need to give him some grace, okay?"

Oliver stares back blankly. His grandfather doesn't understand; this isn't just a hard time for his father. This is who he is.

The nearly daily beatings, the locking him in his room, the verbal abuse.

"Sure, Grandpa, I understand," he replies, putting his head down and staring at his shoes as he walks to the car.

"You know, I'm really proud of you for always getting such good grades in school."

As they drive to school silently, Oliver stares out the window, lost in his thoughts. The car pulls up in front of the school, and Oliver steps onto the sidewalk. Turning back to his grandfather before closing the door, he asks, "How long are you staying?"

"Just a few days. I'll pick you up after school, though. We can go for ice cream or something—whatever you want."

Oliver nods and closes the door, watching his grandfather drive away. Squaring his shoulders, he takes a deep breath, hiding any hint of emotion or sadness from his classmates.

"That does suck. I was really hoping for a break from my dad," he mutters under his breath as he makes his way into the school.

19

CHAPTER NINETEEN

Blake bursts into his office, seething with an overwhelming rage. Last night's surprise visit from his father was like a punch to the gut, leaving him humiliated. He had planned to avoid a conversation about it with him this morning by sneaking out of the house before his father woke up. But as soon as he came out of his room, there sat his father in the living room, calmly waiting for him like a predator stalking its prey. He told him he didn't have time to deal with him this morning, and his father just smiled and nodded. However, as he walked out the door, he stated firmly, "I'll be at your office after I drop off Oliver; we are going to talk."

Everyone in the office parts like the Red Sea as he walks by, clearly trying to get out of his way. At this point, everyone knows not to piss off Blake, or there's hell to pay. And judging by the way he's storming down the halls, he's got some wrath for someone. When he reaches his office, he slams his briefcase onto his desk and saunters over to the window, once again finding himself looking out over the city.

"How dare my father interfere in my life like this. I'm a grown man, perfectly capable of handling how I raise my son and care for my house. The nerve of him to just show up unannounced and try to tell me how to behave," he grumbles.

When a knock sounds at the door, Blake reluctantly calls out, "Come in."

His father enters the office, his expression unreadable. The tension in the room is palpable as they face each other, two generations locked in a silent battle of wills.

"I don't appreciate you sticking your nose where it doesn't belong," Blake snarls, unable to keep the venom out of his voice.

His father remains calm. "And I didn't appreciate seeing my son in that state, or my grandson for that matter."

"Trust me, Dad, you don't want to get involved in this. I don't want to hurt you," Blake growls through gritted teeth.

"Excuse me? Since when do you threaten me?" his father questions in shock.

"It's not a threat dad, it's a warning."

The silence in the room is deafening as the two men stare each other down.

Finally, his father breaks the silence. "I didn't come here to fight with you, Blake. I just want you to get help. You've changed since Katarina died. Oliver needs you."

"I have Oliver under control, Dad. You can go home now," Blake's voice is tight and controlled.

His father hesitates before stating, "I was planning on staying a few days; I told Oliver I would pick him up from school."

Blake pauses, takes a moment, and steps closer to his father, squinting and staring at him intently. "Dad, I'll take care of MY son. I don't need you here."

"Who are you? I thought you woulda been happy to have me visit."

"It's just not a good time, Dad. I'm swamped and have a lot going on. You should've called. We could have made a plan," Blake replies, exasperated, obvious frustration on his face.

Oliver's father looks hurt for a moment before nodding slowly. "I understand, Blake. I just wanted to see you and Oliver. It's been too long." He lets out a heavy sigh, filled with regret.

Blake's expression softens slightly at the genuine sorrow in his father's voice. He rubs a hand over his face. "I appreciate the thought, Dad. I really do, but again, you should have called. I need you to go home."

His father opens his mouth to say something but then thinks better of it and simply nods. Without another word, he slowly makes his way to the door and leaves.

Blake pours himself into his work as the day wears on, pushing the conversation with his father out of his mind. It's over, he's gone back home, and things can now return to how they were.

The sound of Christina's heeled shoes clicking against the tiled floor echoed through the office as she popped her head in. "Blake, your son is on line two," she announced.

Rolling his eyes, Blake snaps back, "Take a message."

"He seems upset, sir."

Blake snatches the phone off the desk with an impatient sigh and barked into the receiver, "What, Oliver? What could you possibly need? I'm at work!"

"I... I know, Dad," Oliver said, his voice shaky with emotion. I'm sorry. It's just that Grandpa was supposed to pick me up from school. But he didn't come, and I walked home, and he isn't here either."

"Oh, that," Blake responded nonchalantly. "Yeah, your grandpa went home."

"What? Why?" Oliver's voice rose with confusion and disappointment. "He said we were going for ice cream. He said he would be here for a couple of days."

Blake sighs, rubbing the bridge of his nose. "I don't know, Oliver. He changed his mind, alright? Now, why don't you just stop worrying about it and get to your homework."

"Alright, Dad," he whispered, swallowing the lump in his throat.

Oliver's shoulders slump as he hangs up the phone, his face visibly sad. He called his dad, worried about his grandpa, only to be told he had left without even saying goodbye.

As he walks through the house, memories flood his mind. He stops in front of a family picture hanging on the wall and looks at it. In the photo, he's sitting on his mom's lap, her loving gaze fixed on him, while his dad stands in the background, watching them both. A pang of longing hits Oliver as he whispers, "I wish you were here, Mom. I sure miss you."

His gaze shifts past the picture and lands on his dad's bedroom door. For a moment, he hesitates. He knows he isn't supposed to go in there, but he can't resist the pull towards her belongings. Slowly, he makes his way inside and heads straight for her closet. Everything is exactly as she had left it when she was alive. He reaches for a sweater, takes it off the hanger, and holds it up to his face, inhaling deeply. It no longer has her scent, but he pretends it does anyway. If he tries really hard, he can still recall it. Carefully hanging it back up, he continues sliding his fingers along her clothes before closing the door and moving to her dresser.

There are four drawers in total, filled with clothes in the top three. But when Oliver opens the bottom drawer, he finds it full of trinkets, papers, and pictures - all a part of her world that she had left behind. He slowly goes through the photographs. There are pictures of him smiling and laughing together with his mom when he was a baby and a young boy. Oliver's fingers trace the outline of her face in one photo, wishing for her presence so strongly it almost hurts.

He shoves everything back into the drawer with a trembling hand and pushes it shut. As he heads to his room, thoughts racing with malice, a searing anger rises in his chest. "I wish it had been him who died," he snarls under his breath before attacking his homework, crumpling papers and scratching out words until his papers have holes and his pencils are broken. Oliver struggles to concentrate as his inner demons consume his mind. He can't shake the image of his father, writhing in pain just like Oliver has for so long. The thought of seeing his father's name etched on a grave marker brings him a twisted sense of satisfaction. But as he always does, he pushes those thoughts down and forces himself to regain composure.

The rest of the day blends together as Blake works tirelessly, and as the sun begins to set, Blake stands alone in the darkened office, the only light source coming from his computer screen. He packs up his belongings slowly, dreading going home and dealing with Oliver. "Although, he should have already fed himself and be in his room reading one of his stupid books by now," he muses.

Blake exits the office building and makes his way to his car. The drive home seems long tonight. As he pulls into the driveway, he notices that all the lights in the house are off, signaling that Oliver is indeed in his room as expected.

Silently slipping through the door, he immediately makes his way to the liquor cabinet. The smooth glass bottles glint in the soft light of the room, beckoning to him. He reaches for one and pours himself a drink, the liquid sloshing gently against the side of the glass. Taking both bottle and glass in hand, he walks purposefully to his bedroom and closes the door behind him with a soft click.

Blake takes a long swig of the drink, relishing the burning sensation that sears down his throat. He sits on the edge of his bed, deep in thought.

He continues to drink, the amber liquid swirling in his glass as he takes another long sip. Gradually, his thoughts begin to quiet. The alcohol courses through him, warming his limbs and loosening his inhibitions. He leans back on his bed, feeling light and carefree as if floating on a cloud.

Something catches in his peripheral vision, and he turns to get a better look. Ever since Katarina's death, he has avoided touching anything that belonged to her. Her closet, dresser, and nightstand have been left untouched. But now, as he gazes at her dresser on the far wall, he notices that one of the drawers is slightly ajar.

As he sits up abruptly, the effects of the alcohol cause him to sway unsteadily. His vision blurs momentarily before he stumbles over to the dresser, his hand reaching out to steady himself on its edge. With a fumbling hand, he pushes the drawer back to a close.

"Oliver!" he shouts angrily. "Get your ass in here now!"

The muffled sound of footsteps echoes down the hall, slowly approaching his room. His bedroom door creaks open just a sliver.

"Dad?" he calls out, uncertainty lacing his voice—Oliver's heart racing in fear.

"Well, get in here! I can't even see you," Blake's booming voice responds.

Slowly, Oliver pushes the door open fully and tentatively steps back, bracing himself for whatever may come. He sees his dad standing next to the dresser he had been rummaging through just a few hours earlier. The moonlight filtering through the window casts a ghostly glow onto his father's face, making him appear almost ethereal. How could he have known? The question pounds in Oliver's mind as he stares at his father in shock and confusion.

"What the hell, Oliver?" Blake's expression is wild with rage as he glares at his son. "I explicitly told you to stay away from her things! Didn't I make myself clear?"

Oliver's heart thunders in his chest as he gazes nervously at the dresser drawer and then back at his father's furious expression. He opens his mouth to speak, but before he can even form a coherent sentence, Blake cuts him off.

"Don't you dare lie to me, boy!" Blake takes an unsteady step forward, looming over his trembling son. "You thought I wouldn't find out? You thought I wouldn't notice that you went through her stuff?"

"I-I'm sorry," Oliver stammers, unable to meet his father's enraged gaze. "I just wanted to see her things..."

Blake's face contorts with even more fury. "Her things? Her things!" he repeats, mocking Oliver's words with venom.

"Please, Dad..." Oliver whispers, his voice barely audible over his father's harsh breathing. "I just... I just wanted to feel close to her."

"What did you touch? What did you take? Answer me, damn it!"

"I didn't take anything, Dad. I swear. I only looked."

"That's a lie. Tell me the truth now or else."

"I'm telling you the truth," Oliver insists, fear and desperation creeping into his voice.

But Blake doesn't listen. He raises a hand to strike his son with the full force of his drunken rage, stumbling and tripping over his own unsteady feet in the process. He crashes to the ground in a heap.

Seizing the opportunity, Oliver darts towards his room, but sensing he doesn't have much time, he turns quickly for the basement door instead. Slamming the door shut and fumbling with the lock in a panic.

"You better run, you little shit," Blake slurs from outside, pounding on the door with his fists. The sound of a clicking echo in his ear as he realizes his mistake. It's been months since he's been locked down here. Lately, his father will just beat him and let him retreat to his own room in the aftermath. The sound of glass breaking echoes through the house as Blake continues to hurl insults and threats at his terrified son.

After what seems like hours, the noise from his raging father finally dies down, and the house falls back into an eerie silence.

Oliver sits on the edge of his father's old bed, its wooden frame creaking under his weight. Musty air fills the basement, a reminder of how long it's been since it's really been used or even cleaned. In one corner stands a stack of boxes, relics from Oliver's mother's childhood that her parents had given them when she died. His father couldn't bear to go through them, so they have been sitting down here all alone, collecting dust for years. Oliver was forbidden from touching them or going through them. But at this point, he doesn't care. Follow the rules; don't follow the rules. He's going to get beat regardless.

With eager hands, Oliver lifts the lid of the first box and finds it filled with books. His mother had always been an avid reader, and her love for books had been passed down to him. Memories flooded back as he remembered her reading to him for hours on end. "Definitely want to go through this box," he murmurs before setting it aside and opening the next one.

Inside were childhood treasures - pictures, art projects, and school awards. Going through these mementos brought Oliver a sense of comfort, like a soothing balm on a sunburn. With slow, gentle care, he carefully sifts through all of the pile of papers and photographs, each one holding a precious memory of his mother. He takes in every detail, tracing his fingers over faded images and handwritten notes. As he looks around at the scattered items surrounding him, a sense of nostalgia washes over him, grateful for these tangible pieces of his mother's life.

Oliver's ears perk up at the faint humming sound, and he turns his head left and right to try to locate its source. He scans the room, moving closer to the air conditioning vent in the corner, but the sound seems to be coming from somewhere else. After a minute of searching, he shrugs and decides it must be something to do with the air conditioner.

Going back to his pile, Oliver carefully gathers up all the scattered items and begins placing them back in the box. The gentle hum that had been faintly present before has grown louder and more persistent and is grating on his nerves. By the time he has finished packing everything up, it's almost unbearable. Frowning in annoyance, he turns his attention back to the box of books, only to realize that the sound is coming from inside. Curiosity overcomes him as he leans closer to investigate. What he finds sitting atop all the other books is an old, worn leather-bound book which catches his attention. It's unlike any other book he's ever seen. He's immediately drawn to it. He takes it out of the box and carries it with him, settling onto the bed, his gaze fixed on the faded cover of the book. Gingerly lifting the cover, he inhales the musty scent of aged pages, and a sense of adventure flutters within him. His fingertips trace along the embossed title, and he carefully opens the book, eager to dive into its world and escape his own reality for a while, knowing that at one point in time, his mother had also read this very book. 'Ancient Histories of the Earth and the Powers Within.

20
CHAPTER TWENTY

Oliver gently opens the old book's cover. As he does, something tumbles out and lands on the floor beside the bed with a soft thump. He leans over the edge to get a better look and sees a smooth stone split in half. "That's where the noise is coming from," he mutters, dropping himself closer to the mysterious object.

The edges of the stone catch and reflect the moonlight coming in through the window, casting small glimmers around the room. It's a simple object, but something about it draws him in, and he can't help but reach for it. As soon as his fingers make contact, a wave of warmth washes over him. Instantly, Oliver is met with a blinding light that engulfs the room. Blinking rapidly to adjust his eyesight, the light tones down until he realizes the stone is emitting a soft, ethereal glow.

His eyes widen in amazement as he gazes at the small, smooth stone resting in his palm. He can't quite comprehend what is happening, but as he holds it in his hand, it's as though all his worries and fears have melted away, leaving only a sense of soothing peace within him.

He places the stone on the bed next to him and turns his attention back to the book. Inside the leather-bound book, Oliver finds a parchment paper with faded writing. He examines it closely, trying to make out the words. He squints in concentration as he slowly reads aloud, "The Stone of Eternal Light."

As he utters those words, the humming stops and is replaced by silence. The room stills, and Oliver's breathing is the only sound remaining. He gazes around the basement; the once musty air now somehow feels fresh and clear.

He looks back at the book and the stone—both seem unremarkable except for the sense of calm that envelops him. "The Stone of Eternal Light," he whispers again, a strange comfort coming from those words.

Turning his attention back to the book, Oliver scans the pages and feels a sense of connection to his mother. This is a part of her, a piece of her that she had left behind for him to find. He traced the words on the page with his finger; for him, he was touching something sacred. Some words are highlighted, and she has notes in the margins.

The hours tick by as Oliver loses himself in the book. The more he reads, the stronger the pull to keep reading and learning becomes. He can feel it in his very bones, calling out, urging him to uncover its secrets.

The book describes a sacred stone bestowed upon a peaceful tribe by Mother Earth herself. The stone symbolized their deep connection to the land and all its abundant gifts. The stone was said to hold immense power, protecting the tribe and bringing them prosperity for many years. But as with all things, greed and ambition eventually shattered their peaceful existence. A violent rift tore through the tribe, dividing them into two factions, each consumed with a burning desire for control over the sacred stone.

As the war raged on, both sides were blinded by their own selfish desires, unable to see the devastating consequences of their actions. Countless lives were lost in the endless battle for ownership of the stone. Until one day, an elder proposed a compromise- split the stone in two. The halves were divided, and they each went their separate ways, unaware that this decision would lead to a dark curse.

It soon became apparent that anytime one side used their half of the stone, the other would suffer from illness and eventual death. The curse was unbreakable unless the two halves were joined together once again. But even faced with this deadly consequence, neither side was willing to give up their power and merge the stones back together.

And so it continued for years, passed down from elder to elder until it became a cycle of thirst for power and fear of death. The once peaceful tribe was now torn apart by greed and stubbornness, unable to see that true power lies in unity rather than division.

In the corner of the page, he noticed a handwritten note he recognized as his mother's. It read: "Never use this stone."

Oliver drops the book onto his chest in utter shock. He looks down at the stone next to him and back to the book, and the realization hits him like a ton of bricks. "This is one half of the stone." His mind is racing as he stares at the ancient book in disbelief. "That's why she was sick, the nosebleeds, the weakness. This is what killed her. And now it's attached to me."

The house is quiet, but Oliver can't sleep. As he lays in bed contemplating the predicament he's now in while staring up at the ceiling, memories of his father begin flooding into his mind. He remembers catching his father in the kitchen, holding a strange stone, and quickly hiding it when he saw Oliver. Another time, when Oliver was young, he had snuck into his parents' bathroom while his dad was showering. He found a hidden stone on the counter tucked underneath a pile of his dad's clothes, but his father stuck his head out of the shower and yelled at him to leave. And then there was that time something fell out of his dad's pocket as they got out of the car. Through the haze of memories, Oliver's heart thumps in his chest as the puzzle pieces begin to click into place. The truth is becoming undeniable- his father held the other half of the stone and, with it, killed his mother. The thought made Oliver tremble with rage. He has to find out for sure. He devises a plan to skip school the next day and search his father's room for the other half of this stone.

Oliver tosses and turns in bed, unable to find a comfortable position. Minutes tick by as he tries to fall asleep, but the feeling is fleeting. After a while, he hears his father's footsteps, followed by the basement door slamming open, jolting him upright.

"Get up, get ready for school. I'm heading to the office; you'll have to walk."

As Oliver rubs the sleep from his eyes and forces himself out of bed, he knows he has to make it look like he's going to school. However, he's determined to find that stone.

Blake pours another cup of coffee and puts his briefcase on the table, preparing to leave. He hears a very faint, constant buzzing coming from down the hall. But because of the headache from the hangover, he barely notices it. He hears Oliver coming out of the basement and entering his room to get dressed for school.

As Blake finishes his coffee, he tries to shake off the lingering effects of his hangover. The buzzing continues but is barely noticeable amidst the background noise of the house.

He furrows his brow as if trying to focus on the sound, but it eludes him. He shrugs it off and sets his mug in the sink before heading out the front door. He doesn't even bother to say goodbye to his son before leaving.

Oliver's heart races as he hears the rumble of his father's car engine. He dashes to the window and anxiously watches as his father pulls out of the driveway. Breathing a sigh of relief, he turns to his bed, lifts the corner of the mattress, and retrieves the hidden weathered book. His fingers tremble as he carefully opens the front cover and removes the small stone, its smooth surface warm against his skin. Tucking it into his pocket, Oliver quickly places the book back in its secret hiding spot and strides with determined steps toward his father's bedroom.

Oliver's heart pounds in his chest as he stands outside his father's bedroom door. He takes a deep breath to steady himself before turning the handle and stepping inside. The room is dimly lit, the curtains drawn shut to keep out the morning sunlight. Oliver quickly scans the space, searching for any sign of the other half of the stone.

He moves through the room carefully, opening drawers and scanning shelves, his hands shaking as he searches his father's belongings. Just as he's about to give up hope, a glint of light catches his attention, and so he turns to his father's bookshelf, and up on the top shelf sits the other half of the stone.

Oliver's breath hitches in his throat as he reaches for it, his fingers brushing against the smooth surface. He pulls out the half he had been carrying in his pocket and holds one in each hand, a sense of power washing over him. He takes great care not to join the two halves together; after all, finding the other half in his father's possessions confirmed that his father did, in fact, kill his mother with his selfish wishes. No, Oliver has something special planned for his dad.

Oliver wraps the newly found half in a small rag, places it in a ziploc bag, and then covers it with another towel before putting it in another bag and tying it securely at the top. He knows that as long as his father doesn't possess his half, he can't make any wishes and therefore can't harm Oliver.

With determination, Oliver walks through the house, looking for a safe place to hide the stone from his father. This is just the beginning of the revenge he plans for his dad and for what he did to his mom.

Taking off the register for the air vent he carefully places the bag inside, and a sense of satisfaction washes over him. "Let the games begin," he smirks, confidently walking back to his room.

As he returns to his room, a plan begins to form in his mind. He knows that he must be cautious and strategic in his next steps. Oliver pulls out a notebook and pen, jotting down ideas and possibilities for the revenge he wants to take out on his father.

Meanwhile, Blake clenches the steering wheel tightly as he drives to the office, his temples throbbing with a headache that refuses to subside. He fishes out a small bottle of pills from his briefcase and pops a couple, hoping they will provide some relief. The buzzing sound he heard at the house earlier this morning still echoes in his mind, making it difficult for him to focus on anything else. It seems vaguely familiar and yet is annoying, like an itch you can't scratch.

As Blake pulls into the office parking lot, he tries to push the nagging buzzing sound out of his mind. He heads inside and greets his coworkers with a forced smile. Throughout the day, he struggles to concentrate on his work. However, he is just out of it today.

In the midst of a group meeting, his usual calm demeanor is replaced with visible frustration and anger. Sensing the tense atmosphere, Axel groans at the boss's agitated state.

"Looks like stress has got you on edge today," he comments wryly. "Don't take your bad day out on the rest of us."

The instant clenching of his jaw and furrowing of his brow only confirm Axel's observation of Blake.

"This is one of those times I wish the stone still worked," he muses, then stops abruptly. He places his hands against the table to steady himself and breathe.

"Blake, are you okay?" Christina's voice breaks through his thoughts, filled with genuine concern.

"I'm fine," he forces out, but the tremble in his hands and the sudden urge to flee betray him. "But I have to go. We will continue this meeting tomorrow."

Rushing to gather his belongings, Blake jogs out the door and to his car. Sliding into the cool leather seat of his car, he shuts the door with a thud and peels out of the parking lot.

"That buzzing sound...it was my stone," he mutters to himself as he speeds back towards his house. "I knew I recognized it." Memories flood back as he recalls how it used to light up and vibrate. "It hasn't worked in years, but now something must have reactivated it."The thought excites him as he pounds on the steering wheel and races towards home—Blake's mind races with possibilities as he speeds down the familiar streets towards his house.

Out of nowhere, a massive wall of dark clouds rolls in, blotting out the once-bright sun and casting an ominous shadow over the landscape. Suddenly, a jagged bolt of white lightning streaks across the sky, briefly illuminating everything in its path before the deafening boom of thunder shakes Blake's car. As if on cue, the heaviest rain he has ever experienced begins to pour down from the sky, pounding against the windshield like bullets. Blake fumbles to turn on his windshield wipers as he slows down his speed, struggling to see through the torrential downpour.

The rain pounds relentlessly on the windshield, creating a deafening noise that drowns out all other sounds. Blake grips the steering wheel tightly, his knuckles turning white as he navigates through the storm. The wind pushes the car, causing it to sway dangerously on the wet road. Lightning flashes overhead, casting eerie shadows.

As he approaches a familiar bend in the road, a sudden lightning bolt strikes a nearby tree, splitting it in half and sending fiery debris scattering everywhere. Blake's heart lurches in his chest as he swerves to avoid the fallen branches, his adrenaline spiking with each near miss.

"Where did this freaking storm even come from? It's like a hurricane!"

With his heart pounding in his chest, Blake struggles to maintain control of the car as he presses on through the violent storm. Thunder continues to rumble overhead, shaking the very ground beneath him.

Just when he thinks the situation can't get any worse, a blinding flash of lightning strikes a tree directly in front of him, causing it to crash onto the road, blocking his path. Blake slams on the brakes, the tires screeching as he slides to a halt just in time to avoid a collision. His heart feels like it's lodged in his throat as he stares dumbfounded at the fallen tree.

In a split-second decision, Blake unbuckles his seatbelt and flings open the car door, the rain instantly soaking him to the bone. Ignoring the thunder and lightning still raging around him, he leaps out of the car and runs over to the fallen tree, adrenaline coursing through his veins. He pushes and pulls at the heavy branches with all his strength, straining against the weight to clear a path. Rainwater rolls down his face, mixing with the sweat of his efforts as he fights to free the road from the obstruction.

Finally, after much struggle, Blake manages to move the object just enough, creating a narrow passage for his car to pass through. Breathing heavily, he hurries back to his vehicle and climbs behind the wheel, his clothes plastered to his skin by the relentless rain.

With shaky hands, he starts the engine and inches the car forward, maneuvering carefully around the fallen tree. The storm shows no signs of abating, but Blake is determined to get home and retrieve his stone.

Yet, as he makes the final turn onto his street, he notices all the houses are dark. "Great, the power's out," he groans, pulling into his driveway.

As he fumbles with his keys to unlock the door, a sudden lightning bolt illuminates the sky, revealing a figure standing on his porch.

"Who's there?" Blake calls out, his voice barely audible over the storm's roar. The figure remains silent, unmoving. Blake takes a hesitant step forward with a pounding heart, squinting through the darkness to try to make out the stranger's face.

The figure on the porch remains shrouded in darkness, its features obscured by the flashes of lightning that intermittently light up the scene. Blake feels uneasy as he stands there, rain pouring down around him, the storm raging on.

Blake takes another cautious step forward, his heart hammering in his chest. "I said, who's there?" he repeats, his voice firmer this time but tinged with an undercurrent of fear.

The figure moves, taking a step closer to Blake. In the dim light provided by another bolt of lightning, he catches a glimpse of a face contorted into a sinister smile. A chill runs down his spine as he recognizes the twisted grin.

Before Blake can react, the figure speaks, sending shivers down his spine. "Hello, Dad."

2I

CHAPTER TWENTY-ONE

"Oliver, why the hell are you home? You should be in school." Blake barks, his face red with anger as he towers over Oliver.

Oliver's grin widens at his father's outburst. "School's out, Dad. Didn't you get the memo?" he retorts, his voice dripping with sarcasm as he steps closer to Blake, unfazed by his father's towering presence.

Blake narrows his eyes at his son. "What are you, stupid? You shouldn't be out here, Oliver. It's not safe," he warns, his tone stern as he reaches out to yank his son inside the house.

But Oliver evades his father's grasp with a quick sidestep, a smirk playing on his lips. "Relax, Dad. I can handle a little storm," he quips, crossing his arms defiantly as he leans against the door frame.

Blake lets out an exasperated sigh, running a hand through his rain-soaked hair. "This is no ordinary storm, Oliver. It came out of..."

"Nowhere," Oliver interrupts. "Oh, trust me, I know, Dad, but you know you're right. We should go inside."

As the duo enters the living room, they are enveloped in pitch-black darkness. The only source of light is the occasional lightning strike that filters through the windows, casting eerie shadows on the walls. Blake turns to his son with anger etched onto his features.

"Oliver, why aren't you in school?" he demands, his voice sharp.

"Don't worry about what I'm doing," Oliver snaps back, his tone defensive.

Blake is surprised at Oliver's reaction. Oliver is not one to snap back at his father.

"What did you just say to me?"

"Don't fucking worry what I'm doing," Oliver says.

"Don't you dare disrespect me, boy," Blake warns. Enraged, he steps forward with his arm raised, ready to strike.

But as his arm almost reaches its target, it abruptly stops mid-air. It begins to twist around unnaturally, like a marionette controlled by an unseen puppet master. Fear creeps into Blake's heart. He drops to his knees, crying out in pain, cradling his arm against his chest.

Oliver begins to circle his father like a shark circling its prey.

As Blake writhes on the floor, clutching his twisted arm in agony, Oliver's expression darkens. He's illuminated by a flash of lightning, casting an eerie light over the scene unfolding before them.

"Oliver, what... what are you doing?" Blake gasps, his voice strained with pain as he struggles with the contortion of his own limb.

Oliver's smirk widens into a sadistic grin as he crouches down to meet his father's gaze. "Just a taste of what's to come, Dad," he purrs, his voice laced with a chilling edge that sends a shiver down Blake's spine.

"What do you mean? What are you talking about?" Blake demands, his voice wavering with a blend of fear and pain.

Oliver's voice is filled with malice as he leans closer to Blake, his smirk twisting into a sinister grin. "You'll see soon enough, Dad," he hisses and taps Blake's shoulder twice, his words dripping with venom as he rises back to his feet.

"What's going on?" Blake pleads, desperation creeping into his voice.

But Oliver remains silent and turns to walk toward his bedroom, the sound of his steps echoing throughout the house.

The darkness makes it difficult for Blake to see anything beyond a few feet. He searches for Oliver's form in the blackness, but he's nowhere to be seen. After waiting a few moments and listening for his son, Blake slowly props himself up and begins to stand. A sharp pain shoots through his arm, causing him to gasp and grit his teeth. It's clear that his arm is broken, the bone jutting out at an unnatural angle. Despite the pain, Blake powers through, determined to get to his room and see if his suspicions are confirmed. Oliver has his stone.

Stumbling through the darkness, Blake fumbles with his cell phone, quickly activating the flashlight feature to guide him. In a panic, he enters his room and goes straight for the bookshelf. His heart sinks as he reaches up to the top shelf and shines the light around, revealing an empty space where the stone used to sit. It was gone, just as he had feared.

Oliver has the stone. An increase of anger mixes with his pain as he collapses onto the edge of his bed. Oliver's ominous words echo in his mind- "You'll see soon enough." What did his son mean by that?

With a heavy hand, he reaches for the bottle of whiskey next to his bed. The cool glass feels familiar and comforting in his grip as he twists off the cap. He brings it to his lips and takes a long, deep swig, savoring the burn and warmth that spreads through his body. The smell of oak and smoke fills the air as he closes his eyes and lets out a deep sigh. "This is really bad," he ruminates as he lifts the bottle once again to his mouth, hoping to drown out some of his physical pain. He continues drinking until the pain is much more bearable and decides he needs to confront his son.

As Blake cautiously stumbles his way through the dark and eerily silent house, the distant rumble of thunder acts as an ominous warning. His thoughts are consumed with memories of all the times he had lost control and abused his son. The shadows seem to dance around him, mocking him for his actions.

"Oliver," Blake's voice filled with desperation and urgency. "We need to talk about this NOW!" Sitting on the edge of his bed, Blake looks down the hall and can make out Oliver's figure slightly.

"Come here, you son of a bitch," Blakes yells as he slams his glass cup in frustration. Glass goes flying all over the place. He winces from the pain. In seconds, he hears someone breathing over him. Blake looks up and sees Oliver. "Oh, you wanna talk about this? What exactly is the 'this' you want to talk about, Dad?" he spits out each word like venom, his body trembling with rage.

Blake begins stammering, "I, I know what you stole from my room. You took my stone, son; give it back! You have no idea what you're dealing with."

But Oliver just laughs, a harsh and bitter sound that makes the hair on the back of Blake's neck stand up. "Oh, Dad, I know more than you can imagine. I know exactly what you did,'" he sneers, looking down at Blake. "And now, you're going to pay."

"What are you talking about? Oliver, what do you think I did?" Blake pleads, his voice trembling.

Oliver stands tall, the weight of his mother's stone tucked securely in his pocket, giving him newfound courage and strength. "I know what you did to Mom," he states firmly.

"What are you talking about? I didn't do anything to your mom!"

"Don't lie to me!"

The storm's intensity grows outside, seemingly in sync with Oliver's emotions.

You killed her!" His accusation cuts through the air like a sharp knife, full of anger and pain.

Blake's expression twists in anguish as he tries to defend himself. "No, no. I loved your mother! I would never have hurt her. I tried to save her," he stammers, his words choked with emotion.

"Liar. Look at you. Even in the midst of all of that's going on here, you still have time to get drunk. You really are a piece of shit. I'm fucking tired of you and your God-forsaken drinking. You know what, I wish the taste or smell of alcohol would make you violently ill," Oliver spats.

"You wish?" Blake whispers, his voice laced with disbelief and fear as he becomes fully aware of what's happening. "Oliver, don't," he pleads, but it's too late. At that moment, he feels something warm and wet trickling down his face. He raises a trembling hand to his nose and touches it gently before pulling it back down. The light from his phone reveals the crimson stain on his fingers. His heart races as panic sets in, and then he doubles over, clutching his stomach as he begins to retch violently. The sound of his vomit hitting the floor echoes through the small room, accompanied by the overwhelming stench of bile and blood.

Blake's vision blurs as he collapses to the floor, his body wracked with sobs and pain. The world around him spins out of control as his son's words echo in his mind. "You killed her!"

Oliver watches his pitiful father, now writhing in pain, on the floor. A small smile forms on Oliver's lips as he ponders all the anguish his father is experiencing. After years of causing such pain to Oliver and his mother, this was long overdue.

I want you to truly see me, to see the fiery rage burning in my soul as I take your life from you slowly, just as you did to my mother. As quickly as the storm had arrived, it dissipated into nothingness, leaving behind a peaceful calm and the warm embrace of sunlight. The rays streamed through the windows and filled every corner of the house, illuminating everything in its path.

The anger in Oliver's voice is evident, "Did you ever think to read the fucking book? To study the stone? Find out about it. Get any kind of information on what you were doing?" The sharpness of his tone cut through the air like a knife. "Or did you just think you found a magic trinket and didn't think there would be any type of consequences?"

"Oliver...please, I don't understand," he manages to choke out, his voice raw and hoarse. "...I bought a book, I read part of it, I just thought it was something special, something that I could use to help me better my life..."

"Mom had the other half of the stone, Dad!" Unlike you, she read the fucking book. She knew the consequences. Every time you made a wish, you were killing her!"

Oliver is yelling, but Blake can't hear him; he's in shock. The dinner and nosebleeds memories come flooding back to Blake. He now understands it wasn't a coincidence every time he wished for her health, she would get worse. He remains silent as he now realizes he killed the love of his life. Oliver sounds muffled."

"I, I, I didn't know! You have to believe me! I loved her." Blake cries in mental anguish.

"Too late for that now, though, isn't it?" Oliver sneers,

taking a step closer to his father. Blake's body shakes with terror as he looks up at his son, seeing only a stranger. "I guess you'll see what those consequences are soon enough. I wonder how many wishes it takes before you die."

"Oliver, please..." The sound of his heaving drowns out Blake's pleading words as he vomits once again. Oliver, with an evil grin on his face, responds to his father's cries. "Don't worry, Dad, I got you," he says mockingly. Oliver grabs Blake's hand and squeezes it.

In an instant, Blake's hand snaps back into its proper shape, and the pain in his stomach disappears. But just as quickly, it's replaced with the familiar sensation of warm liquid trickling from his nose.

"The nosebleeds..." he gasps.

"Exactly," Oliver sneers. "You really are a dipshit."

"But Oliver," Blake exclaimed between ragged breaths. "I had no idea she had the other half of the stone!"

"That changes nothing." Oliver's voice is cold and calculated, like a sharp knife blade. His face is set in a mask of anger and betrayal, mirroring the very emotions that Blake had created in him throughout his entire life. "It doesn't matter if you didn't know, Dad," he said, his voice low and threatening. "You still used it. You still killed her. We won't even mention the torture you put me through. All those times, I went to school with bruises all over. I was treated like an outcast; I was that kid in school. All those years having to bury who I truly am. I'm a fucking psychopath, dad. I love to inflict pain. I love to kill things. I love to cut things open. I'm your fucking son! You knew all this time just who I was. What I was, what I am, and did nothing to help me."

Oliver's empty stare bores into his father, the intensity of his gaze reflecting the brewing storm inside him. "All that changes tonight, you're going to have a taste of your own medicine," he declared with a cold smile, "and I'll make sure you suffer just as much as you made my her suffer."

Blake trembled as he tried to muster an excuse, but Oliver cut him off with a wave of his hand. "Don't bother. I don't care."

Blake begins to stand up. However, Oliver's face twists into a cruel smirk as he utters his next wish. "I wish your bones would break whenever you put weight on them."

As the words leave Oliver's mouth, Blake lets out a shrill scream of pain. His bones start to crack under his body's weight one by one. He tries to crawl away, but the pain is too unbearable. He looks up at his son, showing nothing but regret.

"Oliver, please!" he cries out. "I'm sor....... ahhhhh!!!" Blake cries out from the pain."

"Mistakes have consequences," Oliver growls at his father, his expression offering only anger and betrayal. "They deserve a price. And that price is pain and eventual death."

"No, no, no..." Blake wails as blood begins to stain his shirt from his dripping nose.

But Oliver's heart was made of stone - cold and unyielding. He stood over his father, watching as he writhed in pain, his cries for mercy falling on deaf ears. This was justice, and justice was going to be served.

"I don't want my mother's death to be in vain," Oliver says, his voice low and threatening. "You have so much pain ahead of you."

As Blake shakes with terror and pain, Oliver can see the deep-rooted fear coming from his father—the same fear this so-called man inflicted upon him for years and years.

"I wish for your bones to heal so you can be in mental anguish all night wondering what is coming next, and I wish for all the emotional pain you caused anyone to come back to you tenfold."

With a frustrated huff, Oliver storms into his bedroom and slams the door shut behind him. He can still hear his father's sobs echoing through the house and finds himself instantly annoyed. A satisfied grin spreads across his face as he falls onto his bed with a soft thud. "It was in that moment he realized he fucked up," he chuckles to himself, a sense of joy wash over him like a warm embrace after a cold day.

22

CHAPTER TWENTY-TWO

Oliver doesn't know how long he's been lying in bed, savoring the sweet taste of revenge. But eventually, curiosity gets the better of him. He gets up from his bed, strolling toward his father's room. He hears his father's phone ringing. As he opens the door, he sees his father lying on the floor, staring at the ceiling. His phone is lying on the floor next to him, its screen lighting up with a voicemail notification. Oliver bends down to pick it up and presses play on the speaker to listen to the message.

"Blake, this is Jeremy from Human Resources. We've tried to reach you at your office and have called several times. It's not customary to do this by phone, but effective immediately, you are relieved of your duties at the firm. Someone will contact you to discuss the next steps. The company car will be picked up first thing in the morning. We wish you the best."

Oliver stares back in disgust at his father's pathetic state. "Oh, poor you," he sneers, his voice dripping with sarcasm." Oh, and just in case you were thinking about trying to escape in the dead of night," Oliver's voice is full of malice and control. "I wish you were completely paralyzed, unable even to lift a finger." As soon as the words left his lips, an intense pressure spread throughout Blake's body, rendering him immobile. Panic courses through his mind as he tries desperately to move, but his limbs refuse to obey. "Oh, and I wish for you to replay my mother's death over and over and over. It should just continue on a loop in your thoughts. Haunting you and giving you not a moment of peace. You need to remember constantly what your selfishness did."

Blake groans and closes his eyes tightly. "I could really use some fresh air. I'd invite you to come with me...but..."

Leaving his father on the floor, Oliver walks out of the house and into the cold night air. The city is alive with activity, the streets bustling with people going about their business. But Oliver's mind is solely focused on his vengeance. It's all he can think about, all he needs. He's lived in fear for years, but now he's in control. And he is going to avenge the death of his precious mother.

As Oliver walks silently along the sidewalk, he notices everyone around him. The young man walking and talking with his father. "That could never be me," he thinks sadly. "The older woman walking to her car with a bag of groceries. "My mom will never have the chance." Everyone he saw, living their life, minding their own business, somehow drew up further anger and anguish about how unfair it was. All the dark thoughts and ideas he's had over the years that he suppressed because his Mom taught him to in order to be a good boy are all coming back to the surface. Oliver's mind races with ideas of how to continue his revenge against his father. He knows there are ways to extend his father's suffering even further, and he's determined to explore every possible avenue. Each day that passes will bring new levels of pain and misery for his father until his ultimate death.

After walking for about an hour, Oliver's steps become sluggish and heavy. Exhaustion, caused by his inability to sleep a wink last night, is taking over, so he heads back home.

Pushing open the front door, he lets out a tired chuckle. "Dad, I'm back," he announces sarcastically. "Did you miss me?" But there's no reply. "Well, that's just rude," he jokes to himself. The house is completely silent aside from the creaking floorboards beneath his feet. "I believe it's time for some much-needed rest." His voice trails off as he goes to his bedroom, each step like a monumental effort.

Lying down on his bed, Oliver sinks into the mattress. It's been a long day, and he can't wait to drift off into a deep slumber. "Tomorrow is a new day," he mutters as sleep takes him.

As Oliver sleeps, dreams of his mother haunt him. He sees her smiling face and hears her laughter, but he also sees the pain she endured at the hands of his father. A mix of emotions fills him, including anger and sadness, as he dreams of all the ways he will enact revenge upon his father.

As dawn breaks, Oliver drags himself out of bed, feeling as though a storm had battered him. He staggers to the bathroom, squinting against the bright light filtering through the windows.

As the first rays of dawn creep through the windows, Oliver drags himself out of bed. His body is still exhausted, every muscle aching and protesting. He stumbles to the bathroom, water splashing onto his face as he tries to shake off the grogginess. The hallway is lit, casting long shadows from the furniture along the walls. He makes his way to his father's room and pushes open the door, calling out in a sing-song mocking voice, "Time to wake up, Dad! I have a whole day planned for us. My day, of course, starts with school, but first breakfast!"

But there's no reply. Blake cracks open one eye to glance at

Oliver before closing it again and ignoring the taunting of his son.

Oliver giggles sadistically at his father's defiance, a cold smile playing on his lips. "Well then, suit yourself," he says, mockingly dismissive. He turns on his heels and saunters out of the room, heading toward the kitchen, leaving Blake alone with his thoughts and fate.

The scent of freshly toasted bread and sizzling eggs fill the air as Oliver prepares his breakfast. He eats quickly, and after hastily getting ready for school, he steps out of the house and into the soft morning light. As he walks, a sense of determination settles over him.

But before leaving, Oliver can't help but turn back and whisper, "I wish his bedroom floor was crawling with roaches and ants." A wicked smile spreads across his face as he savors the thought of his father's paralyzed state covered in bugs. The man deserves every bit of misery that comes his way.

Oliver's school day is a blur, and his mind constantly drifts back to his father at home. Every time his father pops into his thoughts, he wishes for some new torment upon him. He wishes for healing, only to follow it up shortly with some type of pain. Oliver finds himself excited to return home from school for the first time in years.

As the last bell of the day rings, Oliver bolts out of the school building, eager to get back. As he approaches his house, he quickens his pace, his heart pounding with anticipation.

Oliver's jaw drops as he catches sight of his father's room. The floor is swarming with insects, roaches, and ants scurrying about wildly, their tiny bodies crawling all over Blake, who can do nothing but press his lips together to keep them from going into his mouth. There is dried blood all over Blake's cheeks, going past his ears into little pools on the floor by his head.

"Oliver!" Blake cries out in agony. "Make them go away!"

"Oh, fine, you're no fun. I thought it would be nice for you to have some friends to play with today while I was gone." As quickly as they arrived, with a simple thought from Oliver, they were gone.

Blake glares at Oliver. "I hope you rot in hell, you little bastard!"

"You first," Oliver smirks with malicious satisfaction.

Blake looks up at his son in rage. "You're insane."

"Insane?" Oliver laughs, tossing his head back. "Perhaps. But I'm not the one who locked up and beat his son. Causing him nothing but misery and pain."

Blake's face reddened, his cheeks flushed with anger. "You think you know what it means to be a parent? To raise a child like you?

Oliver shakes his head, the sound of the words still echoing in his ears. "You know nothing about me."

Blake sputters, his breath coming in short, ragged gasps. "I know enough to know that you're a twisted, vengeful child who's trying to justify his actions by blaming me for everything." He shook his head, disbelief etched on his face. "I'm not the monster here, Oliver. You've become your own worst nightmare."

Oliver scoffs, crossing his arms over his chest. "Oh really? And what would you say that nightmare is?"

Blake hesitates for a moment before responding. "A sadistic, cold-hearted boy who would do anything to get back at his father."

Oliver squares up, anger flaring within him. "And what makes you think that's a nightmare? I want this."

With a confident stride, Oliver exits the room, and his mind starts to wander. "I wish he would regain movement in his body," he thinks. As he walks away, he hears a chorus of groans and sighs of relief coming from his father's room as he can finally move his stiff joints and rub his sore muscles.

As he continues down the hall, the sound of the bathroom door closing inside his father's room sparks an idea in Oliver's mind. He quietly tiptoes back into the room and positions himself by the bathroom door, waiting for the shower door to close. Anticipation builds as he listens to the soothing sounds of water splashing against the tiles.

After a moment, he hears the shower door slide shut and quickly springs into action. With a mischievous grin, Oliver causes the shower door to get stuck, trapping his father inside. As the water temperature rises to scalding levels, screams of pain and shock can be heard from behind the door. Oliver's grin widens at the sound.

Oliver chuckles as he imagines his father's writhing and twisting in the burning water. With a sadistic grin, he thinks, "Rinse off the blood from your nose while you're in there."

Months pass, and Oliver continues to inflict pain and suffering on his father daily. He would heal him only to wish something worse upon him immediately after. As time goes on, Blake's physical body gets weaker and weaker while his mental and emotional faculties get worse and worse.

The moon cast a pale glow through the living room window, illuminating Blake as he lay on the couch. His body is bruised and broken, his mind shattered from months of abuse at the hands of his son. As Oliver enters the room, a sadistic smile twists his features. Blake can see the apparent hatred his son has for him. Knowing there is no coming back from this, he makes the conscious decision and begins to plead with his son, his voice trembling in desperation. "Please, Oliver, you're going to do it anyway," he gasps out, "please just put me out of my misery. Go ahead and kill me now," he begs, "get it over with!"

The silence that follows is deafening as father and son stare at each other.

As Blake's final words echo in the room, Oliver stands there, his heart racing.

Oliver's voice trembles with raw emotion as he kneels beside his dying father. "You did this to yourself," he seethes, venom dripping from every word. "I wish your selfish brain would just give up and stop forcing your lungs to breathe. But before you go, I want you to know I hate you. I will always hate you for what you've done." His fists clenched in anger as he watches his father struggle for each breath, the hatred burning deep within him, matching the fire raging in his heart.

"I'm sorrrr......" Blake's voice trails off as he struggles to take his last breath. His body lay still on the couch, a pool of blood spreading from his nose and staining the fabric. The crimson liquid flows steadily, like a river with no end in sight. It seems to mock the fleetingness of life, a reminder that it can be taken away in an instant.

"I don't forgive you."

With a clenched jaw, Oliver snatches his father's worn wallet from the table and shoves the stone in his pocket before storming out the door. "I'm never using this stupid cursed thing again!"

Oliver gazes at the vast sky above him, taking in the endless shades of blue and white. He closes his eyes and inhales deeply, savoring the newfound freedom coursing through his veins. The crisp air fills his lungs, and he revels in the knowledge that he now has his entire life ahead of him, free to chase his dreams and pursue whatever makes him happy. With a genuine smile, he takes in the beauty of the world around him, grateful for this moment.

EPILOGUE

Ten years later

"I can't believe this house has been on the market for so long. Its charming exterior and cozy interior are simply irresistible," Sheila squeals excitedly as she and her husband walk through the front door.

"Unfortunately, the previous owner's untimely death has made it a tough sell. People don't want to live in a place with a history of strange and suspicious events," the realtor explains with a tinge of sadness. "But it truly is a lovely home, and I'm sure it will bring joy to its new owners. Since it's been on the market for so many years, the price is well below the market value for other homes in the area."

"We'll take it!" Sheila exclaims from the living room, already envisioning their future in this charming house.

"Wait a minute, what is that noise?" Brian asks, furrowing his brow and scanning the room.

"Honey, what noise? I don't hear anything," Sheila replies, puzzled by her husband's sudden concern.

"It's like a strange humming or vibrating sound," Brian mumbles, his curiosity piqued as he follows the noise.

He stops in front of the air conditioning register and crouches down to inspect it. "It seems to be coming from inside here," he says as he twists the locks and removes the cover.

To his surprise, he finds a bag tied together at the top. Unable to resist, he opens the bag and pulls out a towel. As he begins to open the towel, his wife looks visibly concerned.

"Um, babe, maybe you shouldn't touch it. You don't even know what it is."

"It's fine," he mutters as he continues to open the towel. He then sees the ziplock with the stone inside.

A warm and pulsating sensation radiates through his hand and into his body as he reaches in to pick it up. "Oh...I quite like this," he whispers, almost mesmerized by the rock's energy and blinding yellow light. "I definitely like this."

Later that evening, in another part of town, Oliver and his wife sit and enjoy dinner at a fancy restaurant. The soft glow of candlelight reflects off their wine glasses, creating an intimate atmosphere. Suddenly, his wife gasps as she looks at her husband. "Baby, your nose! It's bleeding." At that moment, a wave of dread washes over Oliver. Memories of hiding his father's half of the stone flood his mind- the same stone he never returned for. He reaches for his napkin, places it against his nose, and sighs. "Well, shit."